## ALSO BY JENNIFER B WHITE

*Dead Asleep*

*Otherwise*

*Hummus for the Holidays*

The Witch and the Devil's Son

a novel

Jennifer B. White

acorncap PRESS

oakIVY PUBLISHING

LOS ANGELES, CALIFORNIA

ISBN: 978-0-9847546-0-1
Library of Congress Catalog Number: 2011941831


first edition: 02.05.02
second edition: 10.24.11
*Printed in the USA*


*book design by J. Stewart Huey*


AcornCap Press
a division of OakIvy Publishing
LOS ANGELES, CA

www.oakivy.com
www.acorncappress.com
www.jenniferbwhite.com

*For my best friend.*
*For your help, tenacity and patience.*
*For always being there,*
*even before we met.*

*"Bide the Wiccan Laws we must,*
*in Perfect Love and Perfect Trust.*

*Perfect power holds no might,*
*only love we seek is right.*

*See not with your eyes the visions,*
*use your heart and intuition.*

*Grown from greed, pain and fright,*
*be not fooled to think it sight.*

*And when the demon comes for you,*
*know your faith and keep it true."*

# Chapter
## ❧ *1* ❧

At the end of the long dark hallway, the boy could see lights flickering under the closed door. Stepping over broken bottles and a pile of dirty, discarded clothes, he made his way toward the apartment. Two feet from the door where the numbers 666 were scrawled in red crayon, like the drawings of a small child — or the criminally insane, he  stopped. He heard whispering, deep and low, as if some invisible force had scrambled next to him to speak. Startled, he jumped, looking all around. But, even as adrenaline pumped through his veins and his heart raced wildly, he relished the feeling, savored the excitement.

Rotting boards creaked dangerously beneath him as he shifted his weight. His jaw muscles clenched and unclenched as he strained to hear the small voices. The sounds fluttered like breathing in his ear. Instinctively, he swiped at his head as though a fly were buzzing about.

"Speak louder, I can hardly hear you," he said. The sound of his lone voice echoed in the empty corridor. He looked behind him.

Giggling. In a legion of angelic-sounding voices, they sighed, "Perfect power awaits you."

His smile widened, exposing gleaming white teeth. Was it the many voices of Satan, he wondered? No, Satan's voice would be much stronger, more powerful. His body tingled with anticipation. The voices weren't Satan himself, but they were sent by him.

He threw open the door and walked in.

# Chapter
## 2

Entering the room, he saw a group of fifteen teenage boys sitting in a semi-circle on the soiled floor, enclosed by flickering black candles. In the center stood the high priest, Fabian Osgood. His black robe was tied with a long piece of rope that dangled to the floor. A black cape was draped across his shoulders.

"Should I remind you why we are together?" Osgood asked his congregation. He sipped occasionally from a chalice, his eyes searching each boy out, always evaluating.

"This earth is full of unimaginable riches," he told them. "Everything you want is here, everything is for us to take. We're not animals, left only to our instincts. We are thinking human beings, with the power to take what we want. That's the truth about life. That's all there is. Deny yourselves nothing."

He untied the rope from his waist and held it up. "This rope is strong. If I tie it from the ceiling and hang my body from it, it would support my entire weight. But if I take this rope apart, pulling out each tiny strand, it's nothing — just bits of string. We're like this rope," he said shaking it in his fist. "When we stick together we're strong. We're powerful."

His voice bellowing through the vacant building, he inspired the boys with life lessons, amused them with anecdotes, and read from the *Black Book of Satan*. At times he joked, and the boys laughed. When he became serious, a hush fell across the room like a heavy blanket.

A carafe of liquid was passed around. Ceremoniously, the boys took turns drinking its pungent fluid, feeling its intoxicating effects. The high priest suddenly grew quiet. He looked from face to face, letting the group's sense of anticipated wonder grow before taking a small vial of green, oily liquid from the pocket of his robe. He gazed at it, letting the light from the candles sparkle off the glass. Then he stepped back into the shadows.

Moved by Osgood's words, the boy swayed. His body oscillated, as though the room was pulsating — and he with it. Since he'd entered the room, a perverted smirk had not left his face.

"I understand the need to see dark magic for yourself," the high priest said. "You want to actually feel it, to *know* that it works."

He pulled the cork from the vial. "Magic comes in all forms," he told the group. "Sometimes, it takes only the spoken word to change a situation. Affirmations and declarations are like that. They have the power to heal or destroy. Sometimes you can utter just a phrase and change a person's life forever. But when you want something so incredible, so powerful to happen, it takes more — like joining an ancient spell with a potent potion. Sometimes it takes the climax of hundreds of years of work, perfecting the exact combination of components to summon the dark beast from his home."

The boy listened intently to Osgood's words. His body reacted to the effects of the beverage he'd consumed, and he began feeling euphoric. An almost giddy sensation came over him. His skin prickled with goosebumps.

Suddenly, one by one, the candles were snuffed, until only two remained lit. The smoke of the candles blended with the smoke of the incense, leaving the room in a gray-blue haze.

In a shadowy corner of the room, the high priest raised his arms high, lifting his cloak so that he looked like a giant bat. Holding the vial in his hands, he gave the boys another look at his magic. Then, reverently, he brought the glass to his lips and closed his eyes as he drank, swallowing the green substance in one gulp. He smiled at the group, but only for a moment. Then, his body began convulsing uncontrollably. Sucking in long gasps of air, he coughed and wheezed, clutching his throat.

Within moments, the boys scrambled to their feet, scurrying to get out of the way as the high priest stumbled forward. His tongue, thick and swollen, popped unbridled from his mouth. He fell to the floor, his body bouncing off the filthy carpet like a giant flea. His arms and legs jerked backward and forward, as the convulsions continued to rip through his body. Then, abruptly, he lay still.

The drafty room snuffed out the last of the two candles. The boy stood breathlessly in the silence, staring in the murky darkness at the body on the floor.

A moment or two passed, then, like some preternatural creature arising from the dead, Fabian Osgood stood. His image shifted in the lightless room as he wrapped his cloak around him. "Invoke the voice of Satan," he said. "And you will be heard." He stepped forward.

The boys moved back to give him room. Only one stood where he was. Amazed and exhilarated, desire flooded his body. The drama of the high priest's ceremony made his mind and body reel. He gritted his teeth, eager for an encore.

"Walk in the path of Satan," the priest said, his baritone voice echoing off the graffiti-marred walls. "For perfect power awaits you."

Stunned, the boy fell back several paces. He dug his nails into the palms of his hands. Those were the very words whispered to him in the hallway. "The voices came to me," he uttered to himself, "because I'm the chosen one. Satan prepares the way for me." No one heard him. No one looked at him.

All eyes were fixed on Osgood who said, "Satan prepares the way for us."

In the blackness of the room, the boy smiled to himself. The coincidences were too strong. Whatever wickedness was at play, he was to be a part of it. It was an offering, and he humbly accepted. "I walk in the path of Satan," he said. Somewhere, he was sure, someone was listening.

# Chapter
## 3

With wind-burned cheeks and icy hands, Melody pushed through the end of the wheat field, running the rest of the way home. Home was a two hundred year-old farmhouse with a wrap-around porch, built by her great-grandfather. The white paint was chipping badly and the house was missing two black shutters on the front. There was always something in need of repair around home — a leaky roof, a broken screen door — but it was always clean and it often smelled of delicious things cooking.

As she approached the back porch, a chicken moved across the yard and began pecking at her feet, looking for the corn she usually threw. "Stop it, Annabelle," Melody said, lifting her foot and nudging the chicken away.

Inside, Melody smelled bacon. On Ostara, and most of their holidays, Grandpa made a big breakfast with scrambled eggs, hashbrowns, toast, sausage and bacon. A "heart-attack breakfast" he called it, on account of all of the cholesterol. But it tasted great.

"Make sure mine are really, really crispy, Gramps," Melody said looking over her grandfather's shoulder and kissing him on his weathered, tan cheek. He was turning thick strips of bacon.

"Who says there's enough here for you, now, eh?" Earl Blackstone asked, his gentle voice thick with a Midwestern drawl.

"And I want my eggs poached, not scrambled," Melody continued.

"Oh yeah? Well Annabelle didn't lay enough eggs for you," he said with a chuckle. "Said you weren't spending enough time with her lately, so she was plum done making eggs for your holidays."

Melody adjusted a cushion on the old pine ladderback chair and seated herself at the kitchen table.

"Well, reckon you're too skinny anyway," Earl decided. "Maybe I'd better be giving you *my* bacon and eggs just to fatten you up."

Melody smiled at her grandfather. "That's right Gramps. There's only enough there for one Sumo wrestler." She paused, adding, "You know, the flowers were there again."

"Yup," Earl said, poking at the bacon. "Sure's a mystery. Whoever it is, they ain't missed a holiday these past coupla years."

"Well, at some point soon, I'm going to catch them."

"Think so, hmm?"

"Yup. I'm going to get up really early and go down to the altar and wait for them," she said matter-of-factly.

"Um. But, weren't you there pretty early this morning? Thought you got up with the sun."

"Yeah, but, obviously I wasn't up early *enough*. Next time..." she resolved, gazing out the window. She wondered who else was using the ancient stone altar hidden in the windbreak of her family's wheat field. As far as she knew, she, her mother, and her grandfather, were the only Wiccans in Welbourne, maybe even in all of Cowley County. Yet, for almost two years, at every Wiccan holiday, meadow flowers mysteriously appeared on the altar.

"Is mom up, yet?" she asked, getting up to set the table for breakfast.

"She was gettin' dressed when I came downstairs," Earl said. He tossed several pieces of wheat bread into the toaster oven, then began cracking eggs into a bowl.

"Is she working today?" Melody asked, then shook her head. "Forget it," she said bitterly. "I already know the answer."

Earl grumbled under his breath. "Has to. The diner's been short-staffed."

Like a cloud passing over the sun, Melody's expression turned gloomy.

Earl assessed his sixteen-year-old granddaughter. She took after his German side of the family, tall and wiry, with a wild mop of straw-colored hair hanging straight down, mid-back. Freckles dotted her fair complexion.

"Here she is," Melody said as her mother, clogs clomping on the linoleum, entered the room.

Leotie was wearing a tan waitress uniform with a laminated name-tag pinned to it. A yellow smiley-face sticker, half peeled off, was stuck to a corner of the pin. Aside from her height, Leotie was physically a lot different from her fair-skinned daughter. Her Kiowa, Native American ancestry showed itself in her high cheekbones and smooth, dark complexion. She also had a little Irish, Scottish and, like her daughter, a little German in her blood, making for interesting, attractive features.

"Well, I hope you've been talking nice about me," Leotie said, her tawny brown eyes sparkling. Her thick black hair was pulled off her face in a bun, little wisps of hair escaping to frame her heart-shaped face with curly tendrils. She reached behind her, struggling with the zipper of her waitress uniform. "Fix this, hon," she said turning her back to Melody, who zipped her mother's dress easily.

"Why do you have to work *today*?" Melody complained. "Can't you tell them it's Ostara?"

Leotie pursed her lips. "I'm sure Frannie would let me take the day off, just because it's the first day of spring," she said sarcastically.

"Well it's a holiday for *us*," Melody protested. Seeing her mother picking up her purse to leave, she quickly changed her complaint. "Well aren't you at least going to eat breakfast with me and Gramps?"

Leotie touched her daughter's cheek affectionately, before she could turn away. "I wish I could, Melody, but I can't. I have to go. I'm running late. And please don't look at me like that. There's nothing I can do about it," she said.

"What about..."

"I'll drop flowers off at the altar and say a prayer on my way home tonight."

"There were flowers already on the altar when I got there, you know."

"Lately, there always are," Leotie said, and breezed out the door.

# Chapter
## 4

After breakfast, Earl went outside to work on his gardening. Melody slipped into her bedroom to shut out the world. She understood that her mother had to work. Ever since her father died, money had been tight. Still, the knot in her stomach tightened. She wanted to stop the anger she felt, but it just wouldn't go away. Why couldn't her mother share a little breakfast with them? It was a holiday! And would one quick trip to the altar really jeopardize her job?

She locked her door, turned the dimmer switch down low, and lit a white candle. Sitting in the middle of her room, she began meditating. She closed her eyes and released three cleansing breaths, trying to relax her head and shoulders, then her entire body. Soon, she'd fall into a deep trance, a state of mind she hoped would eventually let her communicate with her dead father.

Ever since his death, she'd tried desperately to reach him. She wanted to know that he was watching her on the other side. He'd have answers for her, she was sure of it. He could give her advice, counsel her on the problems she was having with the kids at school.

At first Melody was surprised that her father's spirit hadn't visited her. She'd expected him to come to her, maybe sometime in the middle of the night, or even in a dream. But that hadn't happened. Her dreams about him were always nondescript and meaningless, and she was becoming frustrated. It should've been easier. She figured witches should be able to communicate with the dead.

Her mother felt differently. She worried that Melody spent too much time searching for her father, and asked her to stop. She warned her against necromancy, saying it was important for her to cherish her memories but that she had to go on living. That infuriated Melody. If anyone could understand what she was going through, it should have been her mother. That was when Melody began pulling away and stopped sharing her personal feelings with her mom.

It was her father who'd taught her how to mediate. They used to sit opposite each other in Buddhist fashion, with their legs crossed, palms turned up. Once, when Melody was about twelve years old, she put herself in a deep trance. She'd wanted to know her future, specifically a glimpse of her Handfasting, or Wiccan wedding day.

As her heartbeat slowed and her breathing turned shallow and rhythmic, Melody was rushed into a different plane. Like swimming in a dark ocean, she moved her arms and legs, pushing her body towards the surface. When she emerged, she was standing in a meadow. It was summertime and the wild flowers bloomed shocks of purple, yellow and red. A gust of wind rustled Melody's chiffon gown and threatened to release the crown of flowers from her head.

She stood outside a circle of people who looked at her with anticipation. It was her wedding day and the Wiccan ritual began with a circle casting, sanctifying the meadow for the ceremony. In the center stood a woman and two men. She couldn't see the face of the man to the right, but she assumed he was her groom and the other two, a Wiccan High Priest and Priestess.

The air was sultry and Melody could almost taste the honeysuckle floating in the breeze. But an apprehensive feeling broke her otherwise joyful mood. Someone was missing. Flustered, she looked around trying to locate the absent person.

An old lady beckoned Melody inside the circle of guests. Melody didn't recognize her, but her kind smile put her at ease.

"Did you lose something?" the old woman asked.

"I don't know," replied Melody. "Where's my mother?"

"Don't worry. She's over there," she answered, pointing to a woman at the edge of the gathering. Melody couldn't see her face, but she sighed with relief. She took two steps toward the circle and then stopped. She looked back at the old lady, panic rising in her throat. "Where's my dad?"

The old lady's expression changed. "Oh, dear," she sighed.

Melody drew closer to the old lady. "I can't begin without him. Where's my dad?"

"Why, he's dead, dear."

"Dead?" Melody cried out, tears bursting from her eyes.

"Of course. You know that, dear. He died years ago. You remember, it was a fight. He was such a good person. It shouldn't have happened. He was just in the wrong place at the wrong time."

Like a bad nightmare, Melody yanked her mind back to reality. She'd opened her terrified eyes, and after a few moments, realized her father was holding her, peering into her face. She'd been screaming and thrashing about.

That day, she'd discovered the awful truth about divination — that when you seek information, you must be prepared to learn bad things, as well as good. Two years later, when her father left one day for work and never returned, there was a part of her that wasn't surprised.

She should have learned her lesson. But after her father's death, her need to contact him overrode the bitterness of that experience, and now, once again, she was trying to force the universe to give up its knowledge. She sat cross-legged and with a little shake of her head, cleared her mind of extraneous thoughts, entering a quiet, still area of herself. She meditated for a while, then slipped easily into a trance.

# Chapter

## 5

Rising to the surface of a new plane, Melody looked around. She was in Welbourne Cemetery. The night was black, but a bright moon was shining.

Someone moved through the graveyard. Melody caught glimpse of a figure darting behind a tombstone. Her heart leapt. It must be her father. It *had* to be. She quickly tried to catch up.

The person rushed through the cemetery and Melody pursued, dodging past stone angels, crosses, and overgrown bushes. She wanted to get a better look, but the individual kept just ahead of her.

Suddenly she stopped. The air was still, lifeless. Melody peered into the shadows, looking all around her. Where did he go?

Something rustled low to the ground, then, from high above a crow made a hoarse cawing. Another crow answered the call.

Then she saw the faceless individual scurry furtively among the dead. It leapt onto a tombstone and dove into the darkness. Abruptly, Melody stopped. Something wasn't right — it was the way the person moved, the height and weight. She didn't have to see a face to know it wasn't her dad. And she didn't have to get closer to accept that whoever it was was dangerous.

Fear gripped her. Trembling, she closed her eyes, trying to will herself back to her bedroom.

A wind blew and the trees moaned and crackled. Melody opened her eyes and looked around the cemetery. Only twenty feet away, back turned toward her, the mysterious character hunched near a grave. Was it a mourner praying in the night?

The body moved rhythmically — forward, then back again. Suddenly, dirt sprayed into the air. Cackling gleefully, someone was digging with bare hands in the earth of an old grave.

Suddenly, she was even closer, watching the prowler's hands as they reached into the earth, clawing up fistfuls of dirt. The knuckles of the hands were a pale, ghostly white as they gripped the soil, attacking the ground. Mud and grime shoved deep beneath the nails. She couldn't see the face, cloaked by the blackness of night and the obscurity of her hazy trance.

"*What are you doing?*" Melody seethed. Her voice cracked at the end of her question. She backed away, bumping into a headstone. Her body vibrated in panic. "*Stop it!* Don't! My *father's* buried in this cemetery!" she cried.

Seeming not to hear, the figure continued digging, laughing and mumbling. Melody looked around. Was anyone else there? The ghoul laughed again, and replied to someone unseen.

"Stop!" she cried again, louder. The figure continued tearing at the ground, tossing dirt around. Still, there was no answer. Melody knew then that she walked the cemetery like a ghost — unseen, unheard. She moved closer to see what grave was being disturbed, then drew back in alarm. The Wiccan symbol of a pentagram was crudely drawn on the tombstone, obscuring the owner's name with its dripping red paint.

She shook all over. What was going on here?

Without looking up, the mysterious person spoke in a dismal, ominous voice. "You'll find out."

A cold wind took Melody's breath away. She shivered, and when she opened her eyes, she was in her bedroom again.

# Chapter

Clouds covered the moon, casting a dark shadow over the mountain of trash and refuse. Debris littered Ashby Dumping — broken bottles, rusted pipes, old machinery, rejected toys. Things that were unwanted, broken, or unused were brought in secret to this area by the railroad tracks by the good citizens of Welbourne who couldn't wait for rubbish collection or didn't want to pay the small fees for discarding non-standard items.

The railroad tracks hummed and buzzed as the Burlington Northern train headed for Wichita. Rudy felt a misting of precipitation on his face and looked into the dark sky. Despite the dismal locale, he smiled happily.

He opened his mouth and stuck out his tongue catching one of the first raindrops as the sky began to loosen. Then he guzzled back the last of his Miller Lite and crushed the can. He had a good buzz going and he didn't want it to fizzle out just yet. If he had to face his old man, he wanted to be good and drunk.

Standing on top of a hill of junk, he pitched the beer can into the air. He hollered and ran as fast as he could down the hill, skittering so as not to fall at the gushy bottom. He liked the freedom of being in a landscape of junk and litter. He could do anything he wanted here and it just — didn't — matter.

Stacey watched Rudy from where she sat on top of a picnic bench next to a rusted metal shed. Rudy had too much energy. It wasn't normal. He was always wired.

Neil sat next to her, picking his nails with a large hunting knife, drinking his fourth beer. Stacey was only on her second.

She thought she'd better catch up to the guys. "You wanna go to the graveyard?" she asked idly.

"What for?" Neil asked, not looking up from his nails.

"Dunno. Something to do."

"It's Sunday," Neil answered with a smirk. "Don't ya know ghosts don't come out on holy nights?" He laughed, amused at his own humor.

Rudy came over just in time to hear. Leaping on top of the picnic table, he snatched up a new can of beer, cracked it open and swallowed a mouthful. "Let's go," he said excitedly.

"Why?" Neil asked.

"It's something to do," he said in a high voice, mimicking Stacey.

"Let's just stay here," Neil said.

"There's nothin' happening here. I'm bored. Come on Stacey, let's me 'n you go." He winked at her, then jumped off the picnic table onto a pile of disintegrating cardboard.

Stacey grabbed her denim jacket and one of the last beers from the twelve-pack. She started following Rudy into the night, then glanced back at Neil. He was still sitting there. Now he was carving up the picnic table.

"Come on, Neil," she called, trying to sound casual, as if she didn't care if he came along or not.

Neil shrugged and slid off the table. He grabbed the last beer and followed.

The cemetery, only a quarter of a mile down the road, was an easy straight path by way of the railroad tracks.

Rudy led the pack. Neil followed Stacey. Though it was chilly outside, she was wearing shorts and he was looking at her shapely legs. Her calves flexed nicely when she walked. If not for Stacey's annoying habits, like that stupid snicker when she laughed and the fact that she talked too much, Neil might have been interested in her. He was kind of interested anyway. But, it'd be a little weird to be with her. After all, she was his friend. And Neil didn't have too many of those. In fact, the only friends he really had were Rudy and Stacey.

Rudy moved with lightening speed, so that half the time, Neil could barely make out the large black teenager ahead. It didn't matter. He knew where he was going. And if Rudy got crazy and decided to take off for someplace else, which wasn't such a far-fetched notion, well that was just fine by him. Neil didn't really want to go to the cemetery. There were a lot of memories buried there in his father's grave.

Stacey peered over her shoulder at Neil. His head was down, his hands jammed into his jeans. She wondered if Neil had any interest in her. She hated the fact that he never gave her any looks, like the kind the guys at school did. Maybe it was because of her reputation. Maybe he didn't want to date a girl who had dated a lot of other guys.

Not that she was what a lot of kids at school thought she was. She'd just had some bad experiences with a few guys who happened to have big mouths. It didn't matter, anyway. She'd already decided to leave this hick town. She wanted to take a bus to Los Angeles. She had a brother who lived there. She could get a job in public relations — she didn't know anything about it, but it sounded like it might be fun. She was sure she could get a good-paying job in no time, if she could just get out of school and away from here.

The tracks turned a corner and the cemetery loomed ahead. It was raining harder now, and Stacey's bleach-blonde hair clung shapelessly to her wet face. Her mascara ran, giving her panda eyes and black tears.

Rudy was already there, running around wildly like a mad dog, dodging tombstones, shouting and hollering. Finally, he perched on one of the headstones and guzzled his beer. He smiled, eyes large and crazy looking, as rain poured down his dark face.

"Stacey, baby!" Rudy shouted. "Come sit next to me," he invited, patting the top of the tombstone.

Stacey brushed the hair out of her eyes and sat next to him. She wondered whose grave they were sitting on, hoping whoever it was didn't mind.

Rudy put an arm around her. He was out of breath and panting. "Do you want to dig up a few graves?" he asked.

Stacey stared at him. She knew better than to take Rudy up on anything. Not even when she thought he was joking. "Not tonight."

"You sure?" he asked in a low voice.

Stacey shivered involuntarily. She was wet and cold and wished she'd never suggested coming to the cemetery. At least at Ashby Dumping she could drink her beers in the shelter of the shed.

"Yeah," she said. "I'm sure."

Rudy laughed. He shook his head, and smacked his leg. "You're right. Too muddy!"

Neil was last to reach the tombstone. Without a jacket, goosebumps covered his arms, but he'd never admit he was cold. "This is stupid," he said, careful not to let his teeth chatter. "I'm goin' home."

Stacey sighed with relief. "Me too," she said, hopping off the headstone.

Rudy studied her with menacing brown eyes. It made her skin crawl.

"I'll walk with you," Stacey said to Neil, her voice sounding small.

"Now why are you babies goin' home?" Rudy teased. "Is it bedtime already?"

"It's raining out, Rudy," Stacey said. "I'm gettin' cold."

"I'm gettin' cold," Rudy mimicked. "It's a beautiful night out!" he cried, throwing his arms out wide and looking up into the sky, blinking in the rain. "A wonderful night to be among the dead."

"You're nuts, man," Neil said. "See ya tomorrow." He turned and headed slowly back along the railroad tracks. Stacey ran behind him to catch up. The rain began to fall harder and faster.

Stacey heard Rudy howling behind them like some nocturnal beast. He was working himself up into a frenzy, she thought, and sure enough, just as a clap of thunder exploded in the sky, Rudy let out a booming roar. Stacey shuddered and hugged herself. Lately, Rudy was giving her the creeps.

"Why do you like hanging out with him?" she asked Neil.

"What do you mean?"

"You know what I mean. He's weird."

"No he's not," he said defensively. "He's a little hyperactive, that's all. Besides, he's fun."

Rudy was his friend — practically the only one he had. So what if he was rude and obnoxious sometimes? He stole, swore, and laughed too loud. And, yeah, he acted a little crazy, too. So what? That's what guys did. Stacey couldn't understand because she was a girl. Still, he was glad she didn't bail on them. He liked being around her.

"Don't you think he's getting worse?" she asked. "He wanted to dig up graves tonight."

"No he didn't. He was just jokin'." Neil shook his head and decided not to talk with Stacey anymore that night. He couldn't afford to challenge Rudy's actions. What if he stopped hanging around him? That'd leave only Stacey.

As if reading his mind, Stacey stopped talking. About twenty minutes later they came to a cornfield. They cut through the field and emerged onto a deserted dirt road. When it forked, they looked at each other for a minute.

Self-consciously, Stacey wiped her thumbs under her eyes and examined the black streaks of make-up. Neil's short black hair looked no different in the rain than in any other type of weather, she thought.

"Well," she said, and waited for a reply. Neil simply looked at her. "I guess I'll see you tomorrow in school," she said, shifting her weight onto a different foot.

"Yeah, unless we both get pneumonia."

Stacey burst into nervous laughter. After an uncomfortable moment, she turned left at the fork in the road and Neil headed right. She turned around to wave at him, but he wasn't looking. She was definitely going to leave for L.A. sometime soon.

# Chapter
## 7

Melody hated school. She'd hated it since junior high school when the kids seemed to get meaner, all but sprouting fangs and horns along with their budding bodies. Every day felt like an endurance test.

"Move your gigantic head," someone behind her said, contempt in his voice.

"What?" Melody asked, turning around to face Peter Fairbanks.

"Your fat head is in the way of the board," he sneered. He chewed the end of his pencil, digging his teeth deep into the wood like a beaver that had just found the perfect birch tree. "Can't you change seats, or something?"

Feeling her face grow red and hot, Melody meekly turned around in her seat. She slumped into her desk, allowing the bully behind her a clear view of the chalkboard. She wished she could come up with fast, clever retorts when some jerk like Fairbanks made a crack, but her mind always went blank when she got flustered with humiliation.

As much as she hated them, she was used to her classmate's teasing and pranks. When she wasn't being harassed, she was ignored, and that felt just as bad. To most of the students at Welbourne High, she was an aberration, someone peculiar they didn't bother trying to get to know or understand.

She felt something hit her in the back of her head. Groping her hair, she pulled out a piece of wadded up paper. Mortified, she realized that someone had hucked a spitball into her hair. She spun around in her chair and saw a dozen students snickering.

"What are you looking at, witch?" Peter taunted.

"That was real mature, Fairbanks," Melody sputtered. She turned back around, her heart pounding with anger and embarrassment.

"Is there a problem?" Ms. Harell asked, turning her attention on Melody when it was too late to help and could only make things worse. She loomed over Melody, tapping her foot impatiently. Annoyed, she pushed her eyeglasses back on her face and waited for an answer.

"No problem," Melody whispered. She picked up her pen and doodled on her notebook, hoping her Biology teacher would stop staring. She knew her face had blown up like a big red cherry. A giggle at the back of the class reminded Melody that she was the sophomore class's favorite scapegoat.

Ms. Harell cleared her voice and straightened her suit jacket. "Ms. Blackstone, I won't tolerate disturbances in my class," she warned, and turned to address the class. "If any of you want to make a nuisance of yourself, you're welcome to do it. Of course, you'll receive an F for the quarter. Understood?"

Feet scuffled and sounds of begrudging agreement were heard. Students kept their gazes down, trying to avoid confrontation.

"I'm passing out a homework assignment. The school website is down and the photocopy machine is broken again, so there are just a few copies. I want you to write down the assignment and pass it behind you."

Ms. Harell passed out several sheets of blue paper. Students hurriedly jotted down the assignment and passed the paper behind them. Melody watched the clock. It was close to the end of class and Maureen Mullen, sitting directly in front of her, was writing as if she had all the time in the world.

Melody shifted anxiously in her seat. She couldn't be late for her next class. Mr. Chin's specialty was embarrassing latecomers — and she wasn't prepared to be humiliated in front of her peers one more time.

"Maureen?" Melody said, tapping the girl on the shoulder.

An attractive girl with lustrous blonde hair turned around, her pretty face pinched in a scowl. "What?" she hissed.

Melody hesitated. Maureen had been crowned "most popular" in their class two years in a row. She was the only girl Melody knew who'd seemed to skip the gawky stage of adolescence. Melody felt a stab of resentment, and color rose in her face. She was certain Maureen didn't like her. Why would she? She had a beautiful face and lots of friends. Even the teachers let her coast through their classes.

And Melody was an outcast.

"Can you hurry up?" Melody asked. She tapped her pencil nervously on the desk.

Maureen moaned, turned back around, and continued to copy her assignment from the blue paper.

As the moments ticked away, Melody's patience was wearing out. Maureen seemed to be taking extra care to dot her i's and cross her t's. Melody was certain she was doing it on purpose. "Maureen?" she whispered. Several students looked up at them. "The class is almost over. Pass the assignment back."

Maureen's hands came up to her head, rubbing her temples. "You're giving me a headache," she accused. After a moment she picked up her pencil again and resumed writing. Finally, she turned back around and handed the blue sheet of paper to Melody.

Melody snatched the sheet from her hand and began copying furiously. She glanced back up to see Maureen holding her face in her hands. Maybe the girl really did have a headache, a bad one too, from the way she was massaging her forehead. 'Too much hairspray,' she told herself snidely. She thought about the herbal remedy she had in her pocketbook, a concoction her grandfather had made. It worked wonders on headaches. Melody contemplated offering some, but when she considered the derogatory remarks she'd most likely get, decided against it.

Fairbanks dropped his pencil. Melody heard it click to the floor, and smiled. Turning around, she handed the assignment to Peter, whose head was on his desk. She was sure he'd fallen asleep. Bending over, she retrieved the chewed-up pencil and stuck it into her backpack — a souvenir for a little trick later.

The bell rang, and Melody made a beeline for her locker. Her hands shook as she tried to remember the locker combination. She gave the metal door a swift kick and felt it buckle. Looking down, she saw a good size dent in the door.

"Good thing Principal Fitzgibbon didn't see that," Logan said as he approached his locker, two down from hers.

Seeing a friendly face, Melody sighed with relief. Their lockers were close to the principal's office, and all year the two dodged Fitzgibbon's hawk-like eyes. Simply because they were in the direct line of vision of his office, Fitzgibbon seemed to notice anything they did that was outside the lines of good behavior. Logan had been reprimanded on two occasions for "cussing," and Melody had been sent home once because her skirt was too short.

Melody groaned.

"Having a bad day?" Logan asked.

"Only when I'm *here*," she answered, turning to scrutinize him. She ran her eyes up and down him, looking suspiciously at his new tan khakis and expensive Polo shirt. "*What* are you *wearing*?" she asked.

"What do you mean?" Logan stammered, hurriedly pulling out several text books and notebooks, then slamming his locker shut.

"What happened to your ratty jeans and concert T-shirts?" Melody was sure he was trying to impress a certain red-haired somebody who sat next to him in History.

She hated to admit it, but Logan looked a lot better dressed this way. Before his transformation, he'd show up at school with his hair a mess, wearing whatever items of clothing happened to be closest to his bed—whether they were clean or not.

"Haven't you memorized your lock combination yet?" Logan asked, changing the subject. He leaned up against the locker and gave his friend a superior smile.

"Yeah, I know it. I just can't remember it when I get upset," Melody said, her lips trembling. She hated feeling like prey. The kids at school had put her in a box and labeled her a long time ago, and nothing was going to change that. Unless she changed who she really was, like Logan was trying to do.

Logan moved confidently to her locker, cracked his knuckles, then spun the dial around, 2 to the left, 16 to the right, 35 to the left. He lifted up the handle easily and the door opened, exposing dozens of stickers pasted to the side of the locker door. "You know, if Fitzgibbon sees this, you're going to have to pay for damaging school property," he teased.

"Yeah, yeah. Move it," Melody said, pulling out her homework for her next class. As she was yanking out a notebook, someone caught her attention.

She turned around to watch the student walking by. A wistful expression drifted across her face. "There's Van Masterson," she said to Logan, without taking her eyes off the newcomer.

"Yeah," Logan said indifferently. He looked at Melody and seeing the sudden color in her cheeks, smirked. "He's only been here three weeks. So far the girls seem to really like him."

Melody blushed, looking back into her locker. "See what happens when you live in a small town?" she said, riffling through some books. "All it takes is some new kid in town to get everyone talking."

"Yeah, well, he may be a passing phase already."

"What do you mean?"

"There's talk," he said, shrugging. "You know how it is. Anything new is interesting at first. But, he's kind of, I dunno... *intense*, ya know?" Logan peered down the hallway at Van Masterson who seemed to be having a great conversation with Larry Monahan, the sophomore class vice president. The two shared a laugh and slapped each other on the back before Monahan went on his way.

"What do you mean, intense? What's the story with him anyway?"

Logan chuckled. If you want to know more, why don't you just go talk to him," he teased, and headed off for his next class.

Annoyed, Melody sulked, biting her lower lip. She knew Logan knew more about Van Masterson, and that irritated her. He always got the scoop on things before she did.

She cocked the door of her locker to get a clear view of the hallway through the opening. Hidden by the door, she stared at Van as he animatedly discussed something with a teacher. His jeans and black t-shirt made him look like everyone else, yet somehow entirely different. His thick sandy-blonde hair and chiseled cheekbones gave him a devilishly handsome appearance.

Laughter erupted down the corridor. Mr. Fisher, the Chemistry teacher, patted the boy on the arm in a friendly gesture, then Van turned around and headed back down the hallway towards Melody. She quickly faced her locker, pulling out a tattered notebook, examining it as if she was really interested in its contents.

Glancing sideways, Melody watched the stranger as he neared. He had a quality about him that made him almost immediately likable. She understood why people were drawn to him — why he'd become popular from the moment he'd arrived. Still, she wondered what Logan meant by calling him "intense" and "a passing phase."

As the newcomer went by, he looked up, locking eyes with Melody. A smile passed his lips. It was the first time he'd ever *noticed* her. In the three weeks he'd been at Welbourne High, she'd been all but invisible to him. Now, he was actually gazing into her eyes. And in that instant, though she didn't know what or why, she felt that something would transpire between them.

# Chapter
## 8

A dozen fowl gathered around Melody as she tossed feed to the ground. She squatted next to Annabelle, allowing her favorite barn animal to eat from her hand. "See, you can be polite when you want to be," she said to the bird. Two fat white geese interrupted Annabelle's dining, rudely snatching the food from Melody's hand. "That's the problem with you feathered folk. No manners."

She reached into her jacket pocket, pulling out a number two pencil, so badly chewed it barely had any of its original yellow paint left. She crinkled her nose, holding it by the eraser with her thumb and index finger. It was hard not to picture Peter Fairbanks' slimy mouth covering the pencil with germs.

She felt a pang of guilt as she dropped the pencil into a tub of chicken and geese feces. For a moment, she debated not going through with her vindictive incantation. Then, she heard his voice as clear as if he were standing next to her. "Move your fat head." She shivered in anger.

She waved her hand over the pail three times and said, "*A cough, a sneeze and dreams of fright will be companions throughout the night. And by morning, you will find, your cold will keep you far behind.*"

She figured the spell would inflict a nasty cold on Peter Fairbanks, making him miss school for awhile. It was a simple spell. Those were the kind Melody liked the best. They were easy and effective. She looked up, seeing her mother coming across the yard towards the barn. She was wearing her waitress uniform and carrying a fistful of wild flowers.

Melody wondered if she should try and hide the bucket of dung, then decided her mother wouldn't notice the nearly-buried pencil.

"Hello chickies," Leotie said cheerfully to the group. "How are all you ladies today?"

"Do you think the males took offense to that?" Melody asked sarcastically. She scattered more seed across the ground.

"Nah. I bet they're fairly secure in their masculinity," Leotie said with a laugh. She snatched her flowers away from a gander that was trying to eat them. "I'm going to the altar. I never got a chance to yesterday, since I ended up working a double shift. Do you want to come?"

Melody almost declined automatically — her usual response of late. Then, shrugging, she followed her mother.

Beyond a chicken-wire fence was a garden sprouting seedlings. In the summer, her family would harvest cucumbers, lettuce, tomatoes, carrots and other fresh vegetables. In autumn, a crop of pumpkins and blue hubbard squash would abound.

Although Melody and her family didn't celebrate Christmas, they did celebrate Winter Solstice. During the holiday season, Leotie would wrap up the wonderful jams, canned vegetables and dried herbs and give them to the ladies she worked with at the diner and to some of her regular customers.

Past the gardens was the wheat field, where they were headed. In the fall, the wheat would be harvested and sold, giving their family added income they needed to survive.

Breaking the bitter silence, Leotie finally turned to Melody. "You're not angry with me, are you?"

Melody looked up, surprised. She turned her face away again. "For what?"

"For missing out on our ritual — placing the flowers on the altar for Ostara."

Melody didn't answer.

Leotie sighed and moved to hug her daughter, but Melody pulled away. Outward displays of affection had noticeably declined between them since her father's death. So had the arguments, intimate talks, and laughter. In their place was a strange uncomfortableness and grievous silence.

For a while, Melody watched her feet trample the wheat beneath them. She looked back at her mother, and her stomach tightened seeing the sad expression on her face. Why was everything so messed up between them lately? She cleared her throat and asked, "How did you find someone? You know, like dad. Someone you wanted to love forever. Someone who believes what we believe?"

Caught off guard, Leotie looked at Melody whose eyes met hers with a hopeful gaze. She smiled and said, "When it's time, you'll meet the man that's right for you. It's providence," she assured her.

"What's providence?"

"Providence is the caring spirit of the universe. It means that whatever is meant to be will be."

The two were approaching the windbreak in the middle of the wheat field. In the flat plains of Kansas, farmers often planted an island of trees in between fields so that, in the event of a storm, the trees could snag the wind, preventing it from tearing up and destroying the farmer's entire crop. On the Blackstone farm, tall, thin cottonwood trees were planted as a windbreak. At the edge of the windbreak was the altar.

Wilted flowers, scorched by the sun, drooped on the stone slab. Leotie took the dead flowers away, putting them in the straw bag she carried over her shoulder. She placed the fresh bunch on the stone, bowed her head and closed her eyes. Melody did the same. In hushed tones, her mother recited a simple, festive prayer in metered rhyme. It was one that Melody had learned as a little girl. Finally, Leotie looked up and said, "Blessed be." It was what their family always said at the end of a prayer and certain rituals.

Leotie glanced at her daughter and smiled. "Ostara is the time of life's renewal," she said. "You know, I have a feeling that this is the start of new beginnings for us."

# Chapter

Melody kicked her locker. It was becoming a bad habit. She looked over her shoulder toward the principal's office and sighed with relief. No one was around. Fitzgibbon was known for standing outside his office in the mornings, greeting students and teachers and keeping a sharp eye out for trouble.

She was about to take another crack at her locker, when Fitzgibbon came flying out of his office. Melody froze in fear. She wondered if every student had instant anxiety over the possibility of getting in trouble. Then she saw his target — Rudy Noble. Fitzgibbon swooped down on the boy as he walked through the school's front door.

Well, not *every* student was concerned with what the principal thought, she decided, seeing the threatening smirk on Rudy's face as Fitzgibbon approached him. Rudy had a bad reputation. He was the type to kick a puppy or scrape a key across someone's new car, just because he felt like it. Melody was thankful she didn't share any classes with him. Things were hard enough.

She turned back to her locker, spinning the knob and cursing under her breath. She looked up again to see her friend Bevin, smiling widely. Bevin's auburn hair was pulled off her pudgy face in a neat braid. Her cheeks were rosy and she smelled like fresh air from her long walk to school. "Hi there," she said cheerfully. "What's going on?"

Melody motioned towards the principal's office.

Bevin leaned against Melody's locker, watching the confrontation. "What do you think that's all about?" Bevin asked. Rudy was laughing loudly now, resisting the principal's efforts to lead him into the office. Fitzgibbon placed a hand on the boy's arm. Still smiling, Rudy yanked himself away, stepping back two paces.

Melody shrugged. "I don't know. Maybe Fitzgibbon's caught wind of a fight scheduled for after school."

Talking in a low, stern voice, Fitzgibbon gave Rudy a warning. "Either you accompany me to my office right now, Mr. Noble, or I will be forced to have you physically removed from the premises." He took a handkerchief out of his back pocket and ran it over his sweaty face.

Rudy looked up at the old man and smiled. His teeth were unusually white and his smile was menacing. "What for? How come you always blame me for everything? I don't have to do nothing," he said, crossing his arms over his chest.

There was an awkward moment of absolute quiet. Melody and Bevin watched the silent stand-off. Although no one said a word, the two stood dangerously close to one another, their energies focused.

"You know, Mr. Nobel," Fitzgibbon said, breaking the deathly hush, "digging up graves is not only illegal, it's immoral and downright wicked."

Stunned, Melody gasped. She turned to Bevin, who was chewing her fingernails, staring at the altercation. "Did he say digging up graves?" Melody asked, her heart thumping wildly in her chest.

Bevin nodded excitedly. "Yeah! Gross, isn't it?"

In her mind, Melody could see the filthy hands of the graveyard interloper, fingernails caked in mud, digging savagely in the earth. She felt the cold, dark, loneliness of that night. It was a trance, only a trance, she thought, and shivered all over. Please, oh please, don't let it be an omen.

Unexpectedly, Rudy began to sing. Actually, it sounded more like screaming than singing. Melody had no idea what song it was, or who sang it.

A fascinated crowd was collecting near the school's entrance. As more school buses dropped off students, the crowd got bigger and more boisterous. The spectacle was enlivening an otherwise boring Tuesday morning.

As the audience grew, Rudy got louder and more exuberant. He began waving his arms around, stomping and dancing, and the crowd cheered him on.

It was then that Melody noticed Van Masterson. He stood only three feet away, watching the scene with quiet intensity. His gaze moved back and forth across the crowd of students jeering at Rudy, egging him on. From beneath a pile of books, he took out a brown, leather-bound journal and began writing in it.

Fitzgibbon's face was red with fury. He straightened his tie and buttoned his blazer. When the Sheriff and Deputy arrived at the front door, the crowd began to quiet.

Melody was suddenly appreciative of her locker's vantage point. She had a front row seat to the curious spectacle, and for once, she'd be one of the first to get the scoop. She leaned back against her locker and watched as Sheriff Larkin handcuffed an unyielding, still-singing Rudy, and escorted him through the front doors.

As Rudy left, he looked back over his shoulder at the crowd. "Thank you! Thank you! I'll be back, I'm just warming up!" he said and laughed.

Fitzgibbon addressed the students. "Okay, move along. I want everyone in their homerooms within five minutes, or I'm going to start writing slips for detention."

Bevin was already texting someone about the Rudy episode. Melody nudged her, then the two quickly scurried down opposite ends of the building. Sliding into her seat in homeroom, Melody's heart was still pounding fiercely. She didn't know if it was from fear, or excitement. Had she actually seen something in her trance that had really transpired? Was this divination, like when she saw her future wedding day and learned her father would die? She began to feel uneasy. Maybe this was something different.

# Chapter

**10**

Earl Blackstone was sautéing onions in a cast iron skillet. He loved to cook and took great satisfaction in feeding his family wholesome food. Feed your body, feed your soul, he'd say. He seemed deep in thought as he watched the onions caramelizing in a sea of olive oil, sending a sweet scent through the house.

Melody sidled up to her grandfather. She stirred the dandelion greens that were steaming on the stove, then pulled three plates out of the cupboard.

"And how was your day today?" her grandfather asked.

Melody wondered how to answer. In one sense, she wanted to tell her grandfather everything that had happened. He'd probably understand, maybe even have some good advice for her. But, what if he got mad at her for disobeying her mother, trying to communicate with her dead father? Gramps didn't talk much about her dad. Melody thought it was because he was still sad about it. And it was especially hard to deal with because of the way her father died. His death had been violent and unnecessary.

"Okay, I guess," Melody answered with a shrug. She pulled out a turkey potpie from the oven, and carefully served it onto the plates at the counter. She turned around, looking carefully at her grandfather. He was a stocky man, in great shape for his age, with tanned, wrinkled skin from too many years spent working outdoors in the sun. Unaware that Melody was staring at him, Earl continued to stir the onions.

"I found out that one of the kids at school was digging in the cemetery," she said quietly.

Earl paused. He looked at her. "That so?"

"Um. It's kind of weird," she said, trying hard to sound casual. "I guess he was digging up graves. Principal Fitzgibbon tried to talk with him before school started, but they had a fight. Finally the Sheriff came and got him."

"Sounds like quite a scene. Know this boy?" her grandfather asked, raising an eyebrow.

"Not really — just by reputation. His name is Rudy." Melody drained water from the greens and added her grandfather's caramelized onions.

When she was done, she looked back at her grandfather. Her mouth was dry and a knot had started to tighten in her throat. She wanted to tell him about her trance and ask him what he thought it might mean. Could it have something to do with her dad?

"I just can't understand why anyone would do something like that," she said, waiting for her grandfather to offer some insight. She wanted to talk about it, but she also didn't want to worry Gramps. She remembered how he'd cried at her father's funeral. To see such a fearless, confident man sob like a baby somehow made the whole tragedy worse.

"Takes all kinds, Melody," he said without looking up.

Melody was putting three plates piled high with food on the table when her mother joined them. She was dressed casually in a pair of jeans and an oversized sweatshirt. Her hair was pulled back from her face in a small ponytail and her face was scrubbed clean of makeup. She looked youthful and pretty.

"Mmmm," Leotie said smelling the air. "Smells great! My mouth is watering."

The three sat quietly for a while eating the fresh sautéed greens and homemade pie. Earl had warmed dinner rolls in the oven, which he smeared now with melting butter.

Almost to herself, Melody said, "I just don't know why someone would want to dig up a grave."

Exchanging glances with Earl, Leotie asked, "What's this?"

Melody relayed the story she'd told her grandfather. Her mother rolled her eyes. "Now why would this boy do that?" she asked. "It's just terrible to desecrate the home of the dead."

"There's something else I heard," Melody said, "something I've been thinking about all afternoon..."

Leotie put her fork down.

"He painted a pentagram on the gravestone."

Leotie stiffened.

"I thought you might be upset hearing that."

Melody and her family often used a pentagram, a five-pointed star surrounded by a circle, in their rituals and practices. It was an ancient symbol representing protection from evil. In pre-Christian Europe, pentagrams could be seen on people's doors, windows and hearths. People drew strength from it and felt a connectedness with the universe. But no one knew that in Welbourne. If they saw a pentagram, they'd think it was malevolent — and that the witches of Blackstone farm had something to do with it.

"Has anyone said anything to you about this?" Leotie asked.

"No, not yet," Melody answered, but she knew it was only a matter of time. There was something else bothering her, but she was sure she didn't want to share it with her mother and grandfather. Peter Fairbanks hadn't come to school. A rumor was circulating that he was sick with a stomach virus. Melody assumed she was responsible for Peter's malady. That made her feel guilty, but it also gave her a twinge of satisfaction. Both emotions troubled her. She wished she could make a pledge to herself to never to do another spell that her family would disapprove of, but she was afraid she couldn't keep that promise.

Deciding she was done, Melody mixed the leftovers together in one jumbled pile on her plate. "Can I go to my room?" she asked. "I've got a test to study for."

"Of course," Leotie said. "You go on, I'll clean up."

After dinner, while her mother and grandfather talked, Melody closed the door to her bedroom and locked it. Her mother almost never came in without knocking first, but Melody didn't want to take any chances. She looked at the books on her desk. She really did have a test to study for, but she realized that wasn't going to happen. Despite her apprehensions, she was going to meditate and most likely go into a trance again. In her heart, she knew that what she'd seen in her trance the other morning, and what she'd heard at school today were related. Something strange was going on, and she seemed to be connected.

To quell the uneasiness growing inside her, she decided to Cast a Circle, invoking protective powers to keep her from harm.

She set out four white candles, marking the Circle, then lit each one with a book of matches she kept under her bed. Standing for a moment inside the ring of flickering candles, she focused her thoughts, then swiftly began walking clockwise, visualizing energy pouring from her body. After walking the circle three times, she faced north and said, "*I hail to Thee, O Watchtowers of the North to come to this Holy Place and bind it with your powers. I do implore you, O Watchtower to guard and protect this circle of the Goddess. So mote it be!*"

Melody did this in each direction and soon began feeling a sense of peace. After the Circle had been sealed and protected, she was ready to conjure its powers. She said, "*I conjure thee O Circle of Power that you might be a boundary between the world of men and the realm of mighty Spirits. A place of goodness, hope and trust to contain the power I raise herein. I have called upon the Watchtowers of the North, South, East and West to help me in the creation of this Circle. In the Name of the Father God and the Mother Goddess I conjure Thee, O Circle of great Power. As above, so below. The circle is sealed."*

As she sat inside the protection of the glowing lights, a soft breeze seemed to appear out of nowhere, brushing against her hair, caressing her face. She closed her eyes and almost instantly began descending into a trance. The world around her spun away, as she dove deeper into peaceful nothingness.

Opening her eyes, she emerged in a cornfield, just outside a farm. It was dusk, and quiet outside. Somewhere in the distance she heard the cawing of a crow. The air was warm and a gentle gust lifted her hair from her shoulders.

Movement to her right. She turned and watched something small leaping through the field. A rabbit? It was fast and she followed it, breaking into a run. Up ahead, she could see a long brown tail twitching anxiously as it darted through the cornstalks. It's a cat, she realized.

Melody heard someone behind her. Cackling. A cold shiver spasmed through her body. It was the same voice she'd heard in her last trance. That terrible, evil laughter. Was it Rudy? Was he chasing the animal? Instinctively, the feline knew to run. Why was he after it? She didn't want to take her eyes off the animal, but she had to turn around and face the tracker. She stopped, whipping around to face him.

No one was there. She looked all around her. He was gone.

Then she heard a sound so horrible, she froze in terror. The high-pitched screaming of an animal in pain. Melody's hands flew to her ears, pressing tightly against her head. She prayed for it to stop. She searched the cornfield frantically, trying to locate the cat and its pursuer. Gurgling, howling. Then an awful, terrible silence.

# Chapter
## ❧ *11* ❧

I've been in this dried-up town almost four weeks now. The old man is a pain. He wants to know where I'm going and when I'm going to be back. That's a joke. He has no interest in what I'm doing or if I'm ever coming back! As if his lax, pathetic disciplining somehow shows he cares. I know the kind of discipline he showed my father when he was growing up. He's a demented religious crack. Dad used to say the old jerk thought he was such a pious man. Whatever he said came straight from God -- so God forbid you cross him! Then he'd get his big fat-buckled belt and he'd show there was punishment to pay for opposing him. Like to see him try that on me! No wonder dad turned out like he did. The truth is, the guy doesn't even go to church anymore. He's a damn recluse. And I don't even know him. He might as well be a stranger, that's really what he is to me anyway. He watches me. Sometimes, when I'm eating my breakfast, I feel his eyes on me. He thinks I don't know. It's OK, though. I WATCH TOO.

It's worse than the juvie in New York. I hate restrictions on my life. Life is about freedom and indulging the senses. These Puritans have no way of knowing how exhilarating life can be. They've lived in a cave all of their lives--a dark, dreary place without knowledge and magic. And they raise their kids in the same way. It's gone on for generations here.

What I see here is selfishness and greed. They might be a poor bunch of losers, but they still go where the money is. There are too many latch-key kids to count. These kids are growing up without parents, and why? Because ma and pa want to make more money working jobs in Wichita, rather than taking lesser-paying jobs closer to home. These kids have no love, no direction. I can show them the bounty life can serve them. They need leadership. They need me. Those that don't follow will grow up to be losers and have children and perpetuate this pathetic existence.

So far, I've seen one girl here who seems different. Her name's Melody. I don't know what her story is, yet, but it won't be hard to find out. I'm a master at learning people's life secrets.

Anyway, one of the school's large football heroes was on his way to class, oblivious. The big idiot slammed into this girl hard and knocked her backwards. He really sent her flying too, all her books and notes scattered across the hall. When she got up, maybe expecting to hear an apology, all she saw was the back of his big, dumb head. He didn't notice, or care, that he plowed right into her. I call her the ghost. No one sees her. No one reacts to her. It's only when she becomes an annoyance to them that they take notice of her. She's an outcast, not in the popular crowd. Not who I've been looking for, but staying hooked with the popular kids has been harder than I thought it would be. There're so concerned with their precious reputations. Any little thing that might compromise those reputations and BOOM! You're out! Who cares, anyway. They're losers, too. I don't even want them. There's just a bunch of mindless idiots. I'm going to pick and choose who I want. They'll be privileged to be with me! If I have to live here, I will make this world into my own. I am untamed! Magical! I will do exhilarating and rousing things here! I've seen some kids here that might be willing to join me, when the time is right. I'm getting ready to make my move. I have to wait for the right moment, that part is critical. But I can't wait too long. Walpurgisnacht is only a month away, and I want to have things in place for the holiday. I'm determined to make this year different. This time, it's going to work. I can feel it.

Van Masterson, March 29

# Chapter
## ❧*12*❧

Sharing a bag of onion-flavored potato chips, Melody and Bevin watched Van Masterson from where they were sitting at the farthest end of the cafeteria. He was hovering over a table of popular girls, who formed a clique just by virtue of their good looks. Two of the girls laughed, batting their eyelashes. The others seem to divert their gaze, whispering in each other's ears, cautious of who was watching them, concerned for their reputations.

"Look at him," Bevin said. "He's been in school only a month, and he's already gone from being the most popular guy in the sophomore class to becoming almost a pariah." She shoved a handful of potato chips into her mouth. "Can you believe that even Logan tried making friends with him?" she continued with a huff at her friend's traitorous behavior.

"Yeah, well Logan seems to be trying to find ways to make it over to the other side. He's even been trying out a new look. He thinks he can make points with the popular kids." Melody shook her head. "Like anything does us any good with them."

"Yeah, I bet all the money he makes pumping gas goes to his new wardrobe. Whatever happened to saving for college?" Bevin asked.

"I think he's found a new objective."

"I hope you don't mean the girl that sits beside him in History?" Bevin pouted.

"Maybe her... and maybe him," Melody said, gesturing towards Van. The two friends watched him leave the table of popular girls, where he hadn't had much success, and head for the dessert table. He'd only been there a moment when he spotted Larry Monahan. He walked up to him in line, looking for some quick conversation. From where Bevin and Melody sat, it was obvious that Monahan was giving Van the cold shoulder.

"It's sad we have to actually witness this fall from grace," Bevin joked.

"What do you mean?"

"You know. The popular kids don't like him anymore."

Melody pondered Bevin's comment a moment. "I dunno," she said shrugging. "Maybe he's just having a bad day. Maybe..."

"Logan says he's intense."

"I heard."

"There's rumors about him lying about things. And then, there's the way he *watches* people. I don't know, maybe he really is a weirdo."

"That's ridiculous. You can't actually believe what those kids say," Melody said, gesturing towards the table of cheerleader and prom-queen girls. "I mean, they think *we're* weird!"

Bevin and Melody looked at each other for a moment, then laughed out loud.

"What kind of a name is *Van*, anyway?" Bevin asked.

"It's his grandfather's name."

"How did you know that?"

"His grandfather is a friend of my Gramps. Well, they *were* friends. We haven't seen him for almost two years." She paused, then added, "Logan told me Van's father sent him out from New York City to be with his grandfather."

A wistful look drifted across Bevin's face. "New York?" she repeated.

"Yeah," Melody said. "I guess he was worried Van wouldn't have a chance to ever really know him before... you know... the old man died."

"What else did Logan tell you? Does he have any brothers or sisters?"

"Nope. He's an only child."

"See!" Bevin nudged her friend meaningfully. "An only child just like you! Already you have something in common." She laughed, taking a bite of her peanut butter sandwich. "Don't you think he's cute?" she teased. The peanut butter stuck to the roof of her mouth, muffling her words.

Melody didn't answer. She was watching Rudy Noble make his way across the cafeteria towards the lunch line. As he passed, students moved to get out of his way.

"I can't believe *he's* back in school so fast, after what he did," Melody said to Bevin, her tone cross.

"Who?" Bevin asked.

"Rudy Nobel." Melody nodded her head in his direction.

"Well, why not," Bevin said shrugging. "It's not like he killed someone." She gave a little laugh.

"Not funny, Bev."

"I don't get it. You're not Christian. Why do you care if he desecrated 'holy ground?'"

Melody shook her head, thinking of her father buried in Welbourne Cemetery — seeing again those grimy hands clawing in the earth — hearing the cackling voice of the cat killer. She looked at Bevin, wondering whether to tell her about her trances. Sooner or later, she'd have to tell *someone*. "It's just wrong," she said, finally.

"You're mad because of the pentagram stuff," Bevin said matter-of-factly. Peanut butter was stuck on her cheek. Melody decided not to tell her it was there.

"What do you mean? Have you heard anything?" she asked.

"Well, Logan didn't want me to tell you this but..."

"Oh, no. Here it comes."

"No, it's not that bad," Bevin protested. "Just a few girls." She motioned towards the table that Van had been talking to. "They implied that you were involved, because of the pentagram. You know, all the witchcraft stuff," she finished, making quotation marks in the air as she said the word witchcraft.

"As if I hang around Rudy!" Melody protested. "I don't even *know* him. And, I don't want to, for that matter."

"It's just talk, Melody."

Bevin began working her way through a package of Devil Dogs, while Melody shoved the trash from the table into a brown bag. "Well, I'm out of here," she announced.

"Where to?"

"There's something I have to do," Melody said.

"Now?"

"Yeah. I'm going to fake being sick, so can you take notes for me in Geometry? If anyone asks, say I didn't look so good at lunch. Can you do that?"

Bevin looked perplexed. "Uh, sure, okay. Can't you tell me where you're going?"

"Not right now," Melody said and slid from the table. As she headed for the nurses' office she pulled out a stick of black licorice and bit into it. Ever since she was a little girl, the taste of black licorice made her sick. By the time she got to the nurses' office, she'd be good and ready to throw-up.

# Chapter
## 13

Stacey was wondering whether to meet up with Neil and Rudy. But what else was she going to do on a Friday night? Stay home with her parents, listening to them argue all night with the TV turned up way too loud? Her older brother, Daryl, was lucky. He lived on the West Coast. She'd begged him desperately to let her come and live with him. But he didn't want the responsibility. She promised she'd be no trouble, she'd get a job, pay part of the rent. She'd even clean and cook.

"Stay at home with ma and pa," Daryl told her. "It may not be fun, but it's safer than L.A. Besides, you only have two years until you graduate. Then you can do whatever you want."

If he only understood how awful high school was for her — how the boys looked at her, the comments they made. And even worse, how the girls treated her. They were the most vicious. They called her "slut" to her face and made fun of her clothes. Every day was like holding her breath until the bell rang at 2:45 p.m. She'd walk home alone, sometimes taking the railroad tracks, often crying all the way.

Stacey wished her parents were dead, then she wouldn't have to wait to leave Welbourne and do what she wanted to do. She wished it so often, she worried that somehow her wish might come true.

Glass shattered somewhere in the house. The kitchen, maybe? Stacey opened her bedroom door and peered out. Now, it was unusually silent.

Then, she heard sobbing coming from the bathroom. It was happening again. She walked down the hall to the bathroom and knocked on the door.

"Mom?" she called. "Are you okay? Can I come in?"

"Go away," her mother hissed and continued to weep.

Stacey carefully turned the handle to the door and peeked in. Wearing her grimy pink bathrobe with its years of accumulated food stains, her mother was crouched on the cracked linoleum floor. Shattered glass cluttered the sink. A few shards glittered dangerously on the floor.

"I said, GO!" Her mother's voice rose to a shrill. Her face was puffy from crying, and moist with tears. Mucus ran from her nose. She was drunk again.

"Can I help?" Stacey offered in a small voice, though anger was rising in her chest.

Her mother didn't answer.

"Where's dad?"

"Your father? Huh. Who knows? Maybe with that blonde from the A&P." She gave a hollow laugh.

Stacey noticed her mother's hands were bleeding. Keeping the bathroom door wide open, she timidly advanced, careful not to step on broken glass. There was a pungent smell of whiskey in the air.

"I'm just going to pick up the glass here mom," Stacey said cautiously, gathering the sharp splinters and carefully placing them in the palm of her hand.

Her mother got up from the floor and sat on the toilet. She looked at her hands.

When Stacey finished picking up every piece of glass she could find, she dumped them in the small garbage can by the sink and put it outside the door. She wiped her hands on her jeans. Opening the medicine cabinet, she pulled out the hydrogen peroxide bottle and dabbed some onto a wad of toilet paper. "Let me see your hands," she said to her mother.

Her mother stared at her through watery eyes. Suddenly she reached out to smack Stacey. Stacey jumped back, pulling her head back so hard to avoid the strike that she smacked it on the towel rack.

Her mother laughed. "Serves you right," she said, her head bobbing up and down like a doll stuck to a car dashboard. "You always side with your father. He's good for nothing, and you always side with him."

Stacey rubbed the back of her head. A lump was already developing there. She took the toilet paper soaked with hydrogen peroxide, dropped it in her mother's lap, and left.

"Where you going?" her mother bellowed.

"OUT!" Stacey shouted back, marching to her room. She grabbed her jacket and some cash from her sock drawer, shoving it deep into her jeans. Turning to leave, Stacey found her mother in the doorway.

"You're not going anywhere," her mother said pointing a quivering finger.

Stacey shut the door in her mother's face and bolted it. She heard her mother stumble and slide to the floor. Opening her bedroom window, she slipped out, dropping the short distance to the ground. She was off to meet the gang after all.

# Chapter
## ❧14❧

After vomiting in the nurse's office, Melody had been given a pass home. But that's not where she went. As soon as she walked out the school's front door, she went straight to Welbourne Cemetery. She could have waited until school let out, but she wanted to make sure no one would be there, especially Rudy Nobel. She also didn't want anyone to see her there. That would certainly perpetuate rumors about her having something to do with the desecration of that grave.

First she went to her father's grave on the south side. At the bottom of a sloping hill, she easily located his marker. The scorching sun beat down on the barren land. Nothing seemed to want to grow in Welbourne Cemetery. But, near her dad's grave, daisies were blooming. Maybe it was because he was buried at the bottom of a hill, so that rainwater trickled down, soaking the earth. Whatever the reason, it seemed part of a divine kindness to Melody.

She picked several daisies and put them on his marker. His inscription read: Erik Blackstone: Husband, father. You are deeply loved and missed by us all. We will meet again.

Melody laid down on the ground next to his grave, where bits of grass had sprouted. She put her hand up to the cold stone. "Miss you, dad," she said, the words choking in her throat. "It's been almost two years now, and it seems to be getting worse, not better." She looked up at the puffy white clouds moving through the blue sky and pictured him up there somewhere, floating above. "It's been getting weird lately. I've been going into trances. I've had these visions, and..." her voice trailed off. "I don't know what to do about them, or who to tell. Mom and I aren't getting along so well since you died.

"And Gramps... I don't know. I want to talk to him, but I don't want to get him upset." A tear rolled from her eye, sliding down her cheek and falling onto the hard ground.

She stayed by her father's grave longer than she'd expected — sometimes talking out loud to him, sometimes closing her eyes, quietly enjoying the solace. After several hours she finally said good-bye, leaving for the west side of the cemetery in search of the vandalized grave.

She found it easily enough. Someone had tried to scrub away evidence of the damage, leaving behind a ghostly red symbol of a pentagram on the marker. Melody could almost see the figure of the mysterious individual clawing at the ground. She shivered.

The hours she'd spent at the graveyard had passed by quickly and it was getting late. Somehow she thought coming to Welbourne Cemetery would help her interpret her visions — but all it did was confuse her all the more. The desecrated grave was just a grave, with no answers to give, and she still wondered why she was having these visions — what they meant. She'd been exposed to magic and rituals her entire life, but nothing came close to what she was experiencing now.

She zipped up her fleece jacket and started heading out of the cemetery. In the distance, the train rumbled by, making her notice the tracks. She decided to take a short-cut. If she followed the tracks through Ashby Dumping and then cut across the cornfield, she could knock almost fifteen minutes off her time getting home. It seemed like a plan.

# Chapter
## ❧15❧

"What are you doing with that chicken?" Stacey asked, appalled. She stared at the squawking beast in the rusted cage that Rudy was holding.

Rudy laughed. "Good lookin' little Perdue, ain't she?"

Stacey didn't like this. She sat on the picnic table across from Neil and opened another beer. She intended to get drunk tonight.

"Here chicky, chicky, chicky," Rudy sang to the chicken. The bird slid from side to side, trying to get a foothold as Rudy rocked the cage. He moved to the bonfire he'd started in a corroded oil barrel and set the cage down next to it. "I feel like chicken tonight," he said, chuckling, and began warming his hands by the fire.

Stacey eyed Neil over her beer can. He was carving away at the picnic table with his knife again, hardly taking notice of Rudy's antics.

"You're not going to let him toss that chicken into the fire, are you?" Stacey whispered.

Neil looked up, glanced at Rudy and then back at Stacey. "I'm not gonna stop him. It's *his* chicken."

"Really? What makes you so sure?"

Neil shrugged.

Rudy bounded back to the table, kneeling next to Stacey. In an unnatural gesture, he took her hand and began stroking it. Stacey looked anxiously at Neil.

"Stacey," Rudy cooed. "We're going to have lots of fun tonight. You're so beautiful, I want you to be my high priestess!"

"Your what?" Stacey asked, snatching her hand away. She felt her stomach quiver. She wasn't sure if it was from Rudy's peculiar behavior or the strong stench of rot that hovered in the air.

Rudy stood up, arms flung out to the side. "My high priestess. Tonight, we're gonna have some fun. Some excitement for a change! Let's have a ritual!"

"I don't think so," Stacey muttered.

"Oh yes!" Rudy shouted gleefully. He walked inside the metal shed and came out with a large brown paper bag filled with something. He began pulling items out, arranging them on the table, as if they were on display.

"Oh brother," she grumbled.

Rudy continued, unconcerned with Stacey. "These are the things we will need to perform our ritual," he said and pulled out an ornamented copper goblet. "A chalice," Rudy proclaimed. "And black candles, of course."

Rudy went on naming the items from the bag, which included a bell, elixir (more beer), and a sword. The last thing he pulled from the bag was a black robe, which he put on.

"Okay, that's it, what the hell are we doing, Rudy?" Neil asked. "I thought we were going in town tonight, maybe get somethin' to eat. I'm starving."

"You'll eat," Rudy said, smirking.

"I ain't eating no unplucked, worm-infested, barn-yard chicken," Neil shouted.

"Me neither," Stacey agreed and gulped her beer.

Melody heard voices as she walked along the tracks toward Ashby Dumping. It was a dark night, but as she approached, she could see the flicker of light and shadow. Someone had a bonfire going.

She couldn't make out what they were saying, but there were several people at the Dump, shouting and bickering at one another. She was sure she was about to stumble upon something bad.

She quietly ducked into the brush that bordered the tracks. Following the voices, she moved quietly in the same direction, concealed by the cottonwood trees and mulberry bushes that grew thick in the area. Peeking through the brush, she spied Rudy Noble. No surprise. He was wearing what looked like a judge's robe, and was prancing around an old picnic table wielding a sword. A girl she recognized from school, but whose name escaped her, was sitting across from Neil Carey.

Neil, like Rudy, had a penchant for trouble. He'd been kept back in school at least once that Melody knew of, and was known to smoke in the bathrooms and carve his name in school desks. The only reason Melody even knew about Neil was because his father had died not that long ago. Melody understood the heartache that came with losing a parent, and remembered feeling sorry for him. For months, he'd walked around school with a lost, sad expression on his face. His black mop of hair hung greasy in his face and he wore the same clothes without ever washing them. Needless to say, he soon began to stink. It got so bad that Ms. Harell asked Principal Fitzgibbon to remove him from her class.

Fitzgibbon had hurried into her Biology class, his jaw set tight. But, instead of removing Neil, he dismissed the entire class to the cafeteria, where study hall was being held. Confused, the students and Ms. Harell filed out of the classroom. Before Melody left the room, she caught a glimpse of Principal Fitzgibbon kneeling next to Neil, whose head was down on his desk, hair concealing the unhappiness on his face. Fitzgibbon put an arm around the boy and, as much as he was allowed to, hugged him.

The scene caused Melody to excuse herself from Ms. Harell's class and run to the ladies room, where she sat crying in a stall. She wasn't sure if she cried for Neil or for herself.

Now, Neil was carving something into the wooden picnic table he was sitting at, and, as usual, was uninvolved in the activities taking place around him.

"Let's do it!" Rudy exclaimed. He moved to the bonfire and picked up the caged chicken, holding it in up in the air. The chicken squawked as the cage shook back and forth.

"Do what?" Stacey asked. She was on her third beer now and feeling it. She was getting bored with Rudy's game, as she often did. In a minute she was going to pressure Neil into leaving so they could go into town for some Taco Bell.

"Our ritual!" Rudy laughed. The cage continued to rock in his hand.

Neil looked up at him. "Now what? I told you, I'm not eating no chicken!"

Ignoring him, Rudy held the cage up in the air. "Hey, Satan! This one's for you!"

Stacey's mouth dropped open. "What did you just say?" she asked. "Did you say Satan?"

Without a word, Rudy took the chicken out of the cage and held it by its feet. It pecked his hand and tried to right itself, unsuccessfully.

As the sword cut down across the chicken's throat, Melody let out a squeal from the mulberry bushes. Even though she'd lived on a farm her entire life, her family never slaughtered any of the animals they raised. She'd never seen a chicken get its head chopped off. There was so much blood, and the bird continued to twitch and move about long after its head was rolling on the ground. She suddenly needed to get home and make sure Annabelle was safe.

She cupped her mouth, afraid the teenagers might have heard her cry, but the three seemed engrossed in their cult activities, unaware of her presence.

She quickly stepped back several paces from the clearing, cloaking herself further in the darkness of the brush and night. But, just before she moved to leave, Melody glimpsed Rudy catching the chicken's spurting blood in a copper chalice. He raised it to his lips and drank.

# Chapter
## 16

From the roof of a lean-to thirty feet away, Van had a bird's eye view of the Satanic ritual. He enjoyed the drama taking place. It was like watching actors play their parts in a movie — Stacey, the damsel in distress, Neil, the unwitting enabler, and Rudy, the baneful villain. He admired Rudy's perverse and rambunctious behavior and was thrilled by the climax when he chopped off the chicken's head, making Stacey vomit.

But as far as Van was concerned, cutting off a chicken's head was a trite ritual, far too overdone. Of course, these were just novices. It was obvious they were just messing around. They really didn't know anything about Satanism — or about real magic. Van would have a thing or two to teach them.

They were losers, he knew that. But it was a start. No one from the popular circles at school would want to be a part of his scene anyway. At least he knew now who would be in his Grotto.

He watched Melody shrink to the shadows of the brush. He'd been watching her long before she screamed, and was delighted to see the little witch at a Satanic ritual. Comfortably cloaked in darkness and concealed in his hiding place, Van took out his notebook and began to write:

Anyone is susceptible to falling prey to a cult. People think, "not me, I'm too smart." The truth is that being smart is no defense. It's not how intelligent you are, but how needy you are, that matters. The easiest people to recruit are the lost ones: those that have abusive parents, or have recently felt the loss a loved one -- the outcasts. Unseen, undesired, they want to be loved, to be accepted, to be noticed. They are perfect for the picking. Rudy fits the bill. And his friends, too. All of us, at some point, go through hard times. Timing is everything.

Van Masterson, April 2

# Chapter
## ❧17❧

"Don't look at me like that," Melody snapped at Logan. She ran her fingers through her long hair. Catching a knot, she began pulling at the strands, trying to set it free.

"Like what?" Logan asked. He was dipping french fries into ketchup and eating them one by one. Bevin watched the interaction with removed interest, as if she were watching TV.

"Like I'm nuts!" Melody said, finally freeing her matted hair. "Sorry," she said, sighing heavily. "I don't mean to be snappish."

"I don't think you're nuts, Mel, I think you're exhausted. You look like you haven't slept in days."

Melody looked at Bevin who nodded in agreement, noticing the dark circles under her friend's puffy eyes.

"Well, I haven't." Melody dropped her head to her hands. "You don't understand," she said looking from Logan to Bevin. What would they think if she told them that the same night she'd seen Rudy chop the head off a chicken, another cryptic vision had come to her. This time, she hadn't even been meditating. One minute she was getting up from the supper table, on her way to her room, the next minute, she was enveloped in a smoky blue haze.

People moved around her. Once again, she couldn't see faces, but she heard voices. At times there was laughter, then chanting, invocations.

Suddenly she felt the electric jolt of one compelling presence. She sensed he was manipulative, abusive. Evil. Yet she was drawn to him, like a moth to the flame that would surely kill it. People moved all about her. The commotion and chaos made her dizzy. At first, she concentrated, trying desperately to see the faces. Realizing it was useless, she abandoned the effort, instead allowing herself to feel the dark and painful energies surrounding her — loss, abandonment, desperate desire.

Then, just before she was released from the vision, a voice whispered in her ear. "Perfect power awaits you."

She was wondering what all these visions meant when Leotie strolled over to her daughter's booth. She smiled easily, placing three strawberry milkshakes in front of the teenagers and taking away plates of half-eaten hamburgers and cold fries. "We have some great apple pie," she said, winking at the group.

"We're all set, mom," Melody mumbled, her head buried in her arms on the table.

Looking at Logan and Bevin, Leotie said, "I'm glad you kids took her out today. She's been like this since last Friday, brooding and unbearable! I keep telling her to go out and enjoy the Spring air."

"Well, that's what we're here for, Mrs. Blackstone," Logan said. As usual, when it came to parents, Logan was overly polite. It made Melody uncomfortable. Of course, Logan said she did the same thing to everyone else's parents.

"Thank you, Logan," Leotie said. "Just run her around today and bring her back nice and tired so she'll sleep!" She laughed.

Another waitress, wearing a pink uniform with a large silk flower pinned to it, sauntered over. Tish glanced sideways at the booth full of teenagers. "Leotie," she huffed in a thick drawl, "there are *other* customers in this here restaurant. Maybe you could think about filling their empty coffee cups with that pot you're holding." She cinched her lips tightly like a draw-string purse.

Leotie smiled, unaffected by Tish's attitude. She breezed by the uppity waitress, bringing a donut to a customer sitting at the counter. She filled his coffee cup.

Watching Tish, Melody felt the familiar bitterness rise in her chest. Why did people in this town always act like that towards her and her family? When she was young, she heard the whispers. "Devil worshipers," "evil, damned fools." It took her a long time to understand what those words meant, and even longer to get over the hurt of them. Only, she wasn't really over it.

"So, he cut the head off a chicken," Logan whispered to Melody, drawing her back into conversation. "Big deal. It's not like we don't live in a farming community. I mean, cows, chickens... they get slaughtered every day around here." He slurped on his milkshake.

"Well, I wouldn't want to see it," Bevin said sheepishly. She slid her milkshake toward her and took a sip.

"It wasn't just *that*, Logan. It was the other stuff. They were doing ritualistic things."

"And your family doesn't?" Logan asked. "Come on, you're witches! You do all types of rituals. I've been to some, and let me tell you, from an outsider's point of view, it can look pretty strange."

Melody groaned. She knew he didn't understand. What she and her family did were celebrations of life-forces. What she saw at Ashby Dumping was cruelty, not celebration. Now she didn't want to tell Logan about her visions.

The bells above the door jingled, sounding the arrival of a new customer. Melody looked up to see Van Masterson saunter across the threshold, making eye contact with each patron and flashing his perfect smile. She sat up straight and pulled her hair off her face.

Following her line of vision, Logan waved. "Hey, Van, over here," he said.

Van smiled. There she was, the pretty little "ghost" and her loser friends. He was amused. Logan really thought they were buddies. He'd give them all a treat by sitting with them awhile.

Anyway, more stories to learn about, he thought with roguish satisfaction. He made his way over to the table, his careless blonde hair tousled.

"How ya doin'?" Logan greeted Van.

"Great," Van replied. He smiled and nodded at the pudgy girl, Bevin, and then his gaze fell on Melody.

Without warning, Melody blushed. She shifted in her seat, an uncontrollable smile spreading across her face.

"These are my friends, Bevin and Melody," Logan said.

"Nice to meet you," Van said, without taking his eyes off Melody.

"Wanna sit down?" Melody asked. The words rolled off her tongue too quickly.

"Sure," Van said, sliding in the booth next to Melody, facing Logan and Bevin.

"We were just talking about some weird stuff that's been happening down at Ashby Dumping," Bevin said with enthusiasm. Then, catching Melody's icy glare, she lowered her eyes. "Just gossiping. Nothing really."

"Ashby Dumping? Really? What kind of things?" Van asked, his interest piqued.

"Well..." Bevin began.

"It's nothing, really," Melody interrupted.

"It's okay, Mel, Van's cool," Logan said. He recounted Melody's story, embellishing certain aspects to make it sound as exciting as possible.

"Sounds weird," Van said. "And kinda cool. I wouldn't mind having a look around there. What do ya think?" he asked, looking straight at Melody, who blushed again.

"Well, I'm not goin'," Bevin said. "My mom would kill me if she found out. I'm not supposed to go there."

Melody looked down at her hands. "I'm really not supposed to go there either," she said self-consciously.

Logan scanned Van for a reaction, thinking his friends sounded like a wimpy bunch.

"My grandfather's pretty strict, too," Van said. "But I might check it out sometime, anyway."

Seeing a new person seated at the booth, Leotie strolled over, notepad and pen in hand. "Hello, I don't believe we've met," she said. "I'm Mrs. Blackstone, Melody's mother."

Van stood up, reaching for her hand. "Nice to meet you." His grip was firm and confident, but his level stare made Leotie feel uneasy, as though she were being evaluated. Or challenged. Perhaps both. "What did you say your name was?" she asked.

"Van Masterson," he replied politely.

Leotie stared at him a moment. She could see a resemblance, especially the eyes. "You must be..."

"He's my grandfather. Same name, of course."

"Well tell him hello for me. Can I get you something to eat?"

"No thanks," Van said, sitting down. "But, do you do take-out? I've been meaning to come in here to pick up a menu."

"Sure. Let me get you one," Leotie said, and left.

Melody watched her mother closely. Despite herself, she wanted her to like Van, but her mother gave no sign of being impressed. She came back with a paper menu that read, *The Piggy Diner: 'Stuff Yourself with Good Eats.'*

"It was nice to meet you. I'm sure we'll be seeing you again," she said to Van, handing him the menu and quickly turned on her heels.

As she restocked the napkin holders, Leotie watched the teenagers. Melody seemed smitten with the new boy. She wondered how her grandfather would take the news that Melody was falling for the senior Van Masterson's grandson.

"Your mom's nice," Van told Melody.

"She is?" Melody said, surprised.

"Sure. She seems... uh ...down to earth."

Melody gave an uneasy laugh. "Yeah, she's okay. We've just had our issues lately... yah know?"

"Yeah," Van said, thinking of his father. "I can relate."

The conversation at the table grew spirited. They talked about where Van came from — New York City. He told them he used to hang out with his friends late into the nights. The hot dogs were the best in New York. He ate them smothered in sauerkraut and mustard. He'd been to musicals on Broadway, and seen back-alley street fights. He loved the hustle and bustle of the city. At any time, day or night, there were people out.

The more he talked, the more intriguing his stories became. Almost too amazing to believe. He talked about tagging buildings and subway cars with his friends; he'd dated models; he was on the V.I.P. list for clubs where he knew the DJs. He could go anywhere he wanted to, whenever he wanted to.

Melody listened intently. Van had a big smile and bright blue eyes. Every now and then, he'd run his hand through his hair, lean back in the booth and laugh. Melody caught a light musky scent of cologne and shivered.

The conversation moved on to Melody's group. What did they like to do? Logan played the trumpet in the school band, and Bevin and Melody sang in the chorus. *Really?* Van looked a little surprised. Melody was a soprano, she had a sweet, clear voice that could hit high C, no problem, Logan said. Van said it was ironic that her mother had named her "Melody," and, as it turned out, she could sing.

What did they do after school? They came to The Piggy a lot. Sometimes they'd go to the video arcade in town, or go to a movie. They had chores. Melody's family had a small operating farm. On the weekends? Sure, they got together. Logan and Bevin went to church on Sundays. No, Melody didn't go to church with them.

Van stared into Melody's eyes for a moment. "I wanna hear you sing sometime," he said in a low voice.

Melody looked away, glancing at Bevin and Logan. Bevin was smirking as she slurped the last drops from her milkshake. Logan, catching the hint of a playful come-on, rolled his eyes.

Van checked the time on his cell phone, then stood up. "It was great talking," he said. "I've gotta go." As Van headed for the door, Melody waved a hand at him from the booth. "Hey!" she called. Van turned around, expectation on his face. "I, uh," she sputtered. "I'll see ya in school," she said quickly, putting her hand down.

"That was smooth," Logan teased.

"I think he likes you," Bevin laughed, wiping her mouth on her paper napkin.

Melody hoped so.

# Chapter
## ❧18❧

The smell of horses and barnyard animals lingered in the still, warm air as Melody and Bevin made their way out to the windbreak in the wheat field.

"How old is this altar?" Bevin asked as they approached the stone pile. It reminded her of a tiny Stonehenge. Two large, thick granite stones had been placed vertically, deep in the earth, and another slab had been placed horizontally on top of them. She pulled herself on top of the altar and let her feet dangle, swinging them back and forth.

"I don't know," Melody said. "It's been here since before my grandfather's time."

"Do you like being a witch?"

Melody paused, thinking. "Sometimes. My mom does. She doesn't seem to mind the stuff that goes with it, though."

"You mean all the things that kids say at school and the mean looks?"

"Yeah, you know."

"Yeah, I know," Bevin said with an awkward smile. She thought about how she hid in the shadows of the girls' locker room to change, and the cruel remarks she often heard about her chubby body.

"Logan gets crap, too," Bevin said. "Like, there's no end to the band geek stuff. You'd think kids would run out of good material! No wonder he's trying to change his look. But... I just don't want him droppin' us if he thinks he fits in better someplace else. You know?"

"I know," Melody said. "But, let's be serious. Do you really see that happening?"

They were quiet for a minute, then Melody smiled at Bevin. "Are you excited?" she asked.

Bevin smirked, nodding her head. "Sure. I've never done a *love* spell before!"

Melody laughed. "Well, this isn't a very sophisticated spell. And we're really not supposed to do this, you know."

"Why?" Bevin asked, amazed. "I thought that's what witches do! You know, cast spells, do rituals."

"It's part of what we do. Mostly, we try to be spiritual people and attune ourselves to the cycles of the earth. But, yeah, we do spells. It's kinda like the way you pray in church, that's all."

Bevin looked perplexed. "So then, what's wrong with a love spell?"

Melody smiled. "Nothing if you're simply asking the universe to send you someone you're supposed to be with, the one that you're destined to love. It's just that you're not supposed to cast spells directly at individuals. See, we believe when you send something out into the world, it comes back to you three-fold. So, if you do something bad to someone, you risk that it'll boomerang and hit you in the back of the head." Melody thought of the illness spell she'd inflicted on Peter Fairbanks and cringed.

"Wouldn't that mean that a love spell would come back to you three-times as strong then?" Bevin asked. "What's wrong with that?"

"It doesn't work like that. We're casting a spell *on* people we know. We're doing it without their knowledge — that's like doing it against their will. That's what's wrong about it."

Bevin nodded. "Maybe we shouldn't do this, then."

Melody looked down at her feet and considered a moment. She remembered the way Van had looked at her, the intensity in his eyes, and that generous smile. After seeing him at The Piggy Diner, she'd been euphoric for days. The problem was, she didn't feel confident enough to win his affections on her own. If she'd been born with her mother's beauty she might have had a chance. But as it was, she figured she had to use whatever tools were available to her.

"No, I wanna do this," Melody said. She looked at the water lily she'd been carrying and brought it to her face, taking in the fragrance. "You know what to do, right?" she asked Bevin.

"Sure," Bevin said.

"Remember, you really have to concentrate on his face, all his features and mannerisms. Then, you have to say his name when I look at you, okay?"

Bevin nodded.

Melody looked at the flower and said, "*The water lily has powers over the heart. We place this flower of grace and beauty in its natural earthly habitat.*"

Bevin took the flower from her friend's hand. Carefully she peeled off a petal and kissed it. "Logan," she whispered, trying to stifle a small giggle. Then, gently folding it, she maneuvered it through the mouth of a plastic bottle of water. Melody did the same. After she kissed the petal, she said, "Van." They took turns until all of the petals were plucked from the flower and floating inside the bottle.

Melody took the bottle from Bevin and closed her eyes. She held it tightly and waved her hand around the top of it. Finally she opened her eyes again. Bevin was watching her intently. She said, "In Russia, there are people who believe that psychics can actually charge water. They use the charged water for curative purposes." She took a long, deep drink from the bottle and handed it to Bevin. "It tastes fine," she said, encouraging Bevin. "Kinda sweet."

Bevin took a sip, swallowed, and then waited. "I don't feel anything," she said.

"Who says you're supposed to, dummy. Just drink it!"

Bevin put the bottle back up to her mouth and gulped. After drinking the water, they sat quietly on top of the altar for a moment. Finally, Melody jumped down and knelt in front of the altar. Head down, she said, "*Gentle goddess, oh peaceful, dove, I cast this spell with heart of love. Bring to me the man I choose, grant this to me or love will lose.*"

Bevin clapped her hands. "Cool!" she said. "How soon does it take effect?"

"I don't know, really. Soon, I guess," Melody said, standing.

Suddenly, Bevin clasped her chest. Her face stricken, she gasped. Melody laughed at Bevin's spirited acting. "Funny," she said. But as she watched her friend, she saw the color quickly wash from her face, like wet paint in the rain.

"Bevin?" Melody asked, her voice sounding thin. She felt the onset of panic as she watched Bevin wheeze and her face contort in pain. "What's wrong?" she screamed, pulling her from the altar.

Bevin slid down without resistance. Her eyes bulged, staring pleadingly at Melody. Her body rigid, she clutched her chest. "My heart!" she cried out. "It hurts!"

Melody laid Bevin down on the ground, frantically looking around, wondering what to do. She reached down and put her arms around the girl, trying to lift her. "Try to get up," she urged Bevin, now lying limply on the ground.

"Now what have you gotten yourself into?" her grandfather asked gruffly, from behind Melody. She whipped around, never so glad to see a scowling face in her life. Earl knelt next to Bevin and put his fingers up to her neck, checking her pulse.

"Oh Gramps!" Melody cried. "I'm sorry! I'm sorry! Is she all right?"

Her grandfather shook his head. He opened Bevin's eyes and looked at her pupils.

"Is she having a heart attack?" Melody asked, tears welling up in her eyes.

"Absolutely not," Earl answered. "She's a young girl! Why would you say that?"

"She said it's her heart!"

Bevin let out a soft cry. Her suffering seemed to diminish. She swallowed and licked her lips. Finally she opened her eyes and croaked, "I think I'm okay now."

Melody sighed with relief and bent over Bevin. "What happened?"

"Dunno," Bevin whispered looking from Melody to her grandfather. "It just hurt so much." She struggled to right herself. Earl leaned down and placed an arm beneath her back. He helped her to a sitting position.

"I don't understand," Melody said, searching her grandfather's face for an answer.

"No, reckon you don't," Earl said. "Thought you might grow out of this, Melody — your casual incantations and spells. I was hopin' you would mature a bit. I been telling you, you have to learn to be judicious when using magic."

He shook his head in disappointment. "You may think that what you did today was just a bit of fun, but as you can see from your friend, these things can be dangerous." He looked at his granddaughter. Embarrassed, she quickly wiped away tears from her eyes. "Gramps, what happened to Bevin just now?"

"Nothing," Earl said, standing up. "There's nothing wrong with her.

"But what about..."

"It was your spell, just your spell. Guess now you know it worked."

# Chapter
## *19*

Rudy took the liquid black eyeliner from the pocket of his jeans and turned to face himself in the mirror. He was dark, even by African-American standards. He had a perfect complexion, smooth and flawless, with a square, sculptured jaw.

The boy's locker room was deserted, thankfully. He didn't want anyone to see him doing this, although he was certain he wanted the world to see the results. He unscrewed the liquid eyeliner and leaned into the mirror, wondering if there'd be any contrast of the makeup against his dark skin and features.

He carefully ran the liquid liner over the top of his eye, letting the brush trail off to the far edges of his face, Cleopatra style. He leaned back, assessing himself in the mirror. It was different. He smiled, his ivory teeth gleaming. He liked it. He worked on the other eye.

He thought of the kids at school, the teachers, his father. This would drive them crazy. His whole life, he'd never been an insider. He never felt that he *belonged*. He didn't know if it was as simple as the color of his skin. There were only a few black kids in and around Welbourne. Maybe it was something else. When he was young, he'd spent a lot of time trying to figure it out, trying desperately to make people like him.

Buddy Farkley jumped into his mind. Rudy was eight years old when Buddy and his friends dared him to put the dead mouse in Mrs. Prinley's mailbox. Rudy remembered how bad he'd felt about it. Mrs. Prinley was a nice lady. From Rudy's eight-year old standpoint, she'd seemed ancient. She had long white hair that she wore in a braid down her back, and little eyeglasses that seemed to suit her tiny frame.

Sometimes Mrs. Prinley made cookies for Rudy, and she let him come over to play with her dog, an old black Lab named Bart. Rudy loved that dog, and he liked having someplace to go after school. It was lonely going home to an empty house.

Buddy put the mouse right in his hand. It was cold and stiff. It stank, too. "Go on," Buddy said, laughing. His freckled face opened wide, revealing a mouthful of twisted teeth that needed braces. "If you want to hang around with us, black boy, you gotta do what we say. Go stick it in her mailbox."

Reluctantly, Rudy held the dead mouse tightly in his hand and ran all the way down the street to Mrs. Prinley's little white house. Meticulously weeded flowers bordered the concrete walk to her front door. Every Christmas, though she was elderly and didn't have anyone to help her, she strung lights on the shrubs in front of her house. She was a kind woman, a good neighbor, and Rudy thought twice before he shoved the mouse into the mailbox. But he did it.

Then, along with the other boys, he hid behind some bushes across the street, and waited. Soon enough the mailman drove up, opened the mailbox and tossed in Mrs. Prinley's mail, driving off without hesitation. Like clockwork, Mrs. Prinley, a sweater wrapped around her shoulder and slippers on her feet, opened her front door and made her way outside, moving carefully to avoid falling. She slowly opened her mailbox and pulled out her mail, along with the dead mouse.

It took her a moment to realize what she had in her hand. Then came the scream. The mail was thrown high into the air, along with the mouse. Astonishingly, when the mouse came down, it landed on her head. She screamed even louder, clutching the smelly thing, then tossing it to the ground.

Behind the bushes, the boys watched and snickered, elbowing each other in praise for such a great prank. Rudy felt a knot in his stomach grow tight and painful. "So, am I in the group now?" he whispered timidly to Buddy.

Buddy gave Rudy a look, as if to say that the dumb black kid didn't even know what a great comedian Bud really was. He looked around at the other boys. "Uh, the answer would be NO!" Then he laughed.

"But you said..." Rudy sputtered.

Still standing by her mailbox, Mrs. Prinley was crying, asking the world who would do such a terrible thing. Suddenly Buddy pushed Rudy out of the bushes. Rudy, who was a little kid at the time, fell backwards and tumbled into plain sight.

From the bushes, Buddy cried out, "There's the kid that did it!" Then the boys ran. They ran as fast as they could, leaving Rudy to stare dumbfounded at the old lady who looked at him in astonished disappointment. Then, like the boys who'd betrayed him, Rudy ran, too.

Too ashamed, he never visited Mrs. Prinley again. But the feelings of betrayal and failure stayed with him like it was yesterday. Mrs. Prinley died when Rudy turned eleven.

Wasted, Rudy thought. A lot of time wasted on people who never would have liked him anyway. Now, of course, he didn't care if they liked him. He didn't want to be a part of their stupid cliques. He didn't want to make friends. He didn't even want to be *like* them. In fact, more than anything else now, he wanted to be different.

He was finished. Welbourne High School was going to think Halloween came early. Rudy laughed out loud.

# Chapter
## ❧20❧

The Sheriff was back again. What now, Melody wondered? She slammed her locker at the same time Logan slammed his.

"What do you think? Rudy again?" Logan asked.

They watched the Sheriff and Deputy shake hands with Fitzgibbon and walk out the front door. Fitzgibbon ran his hand over his bald head, then straightened his wide brown tie. Looking up, he caught eyes with Melody. She fumbled with her books, losing her homework assignment to a gust of wind that rolled in from the front door. The piece of notebook paper fluttered, rose in the breeze and sailed several feet away from her towards Fitzgibbon.

Fitzgibbon quickly moved towards the paper. Before Melody could react, he had the assignment in his hand.

Melody looked at Logan, who shrugged. She walked over to the principal and offered a weak smile.

"Good morning, Ms. Blackstone," Fitzgibbon said, looking carefully at the paper. Melody stiffened, shifting uncomfortably from foot to foot.

"It's my Biology homework," she said. Her face felt hot.

"I can see," Fitzgibbon said, still reviewing it. "Well done. I'm certain Ms. Harell will find it satisfactory."

He paused, looking at Melody. She wondered why he didn't just hand it back to her. She hadn't done anything wrong. Maybe he'd found those dents in her locker. If he'd done a locker search, he could have found all the stickers, too.

"Is something wrong, Ms. Blackstone?" Fitzgibbon asked, handing the assignment back.

"Uh, no." Melody answered. She took the paper and shoved it back into her book. Casually, she shuffled back a few inches.

"I have a question for you," Fitzgibbon said. "Do you know the new boy, Van Masterson?"

Melody blinked. That's what this was all about? "Sure, everyone does. Why?"

"Oh, no particular reason. I just wondered what you knew about him."

"Not much," she shrugged, looking over her shoulder at Logan. He was leaning up against his locker, waiting for her. "He's from New York, he lives with his grandfather. Um, he likes hot dogs with sauerkraut." She giggled nervously.

"I see," Fitzgibbon said.

"I'm sorry, Principal Fitzgibbon," she said. "I probably know as much about him as anyone, which isn't much. He seems nice enough. Uh, is he in trouble or something?"

Fitzgibbon gazed at Melody a moment, making her uneasy. Something definitely was going on, and somehow Fitzgibbon thought she knew something. She couldn't imagine what he was thinking.

"No, Melody, he's not in any trouble. At least not yet. But, you did see that the Sheriff was here again today, didn't you?"

She nodded.

"He was asking me about some of the students. Wondering if I knew anyone who might kill animals — small animals — chickens, rabbits, things of that nature." Fitzgibbon paused, watching Melody's reaction. She was stunned into silence.

"You see, people around town have been reporting animals missing. Some have turned up dead in their owners' yards. And not just livestock or caged rabbits and such, but pets — cats and dogs. Looks like they've been sacrificed."

Melody gasped. "What? Pets?"

"Pets, Ms. Blackstone. You do have a pet, don't you? Can you imagine if, let's say, your puppy Spot turned up skinned, gutted and mutilated on your front porch? It's enough to make you sick, isn't it?"

Melody's hand came up to her mouth. She thought about Rudy and the chicken he'd slain at Ashby Dumping. She remembered all the blood and the crazy look on his face. She'd thought about telling someone, but after talking to Logan and Bevin, they didn't seem to think it was such a terrible thing. In fact, Logan thought it was probably Rudy's own chicken. "Who's to tell someone what to do with their own livestock?" he'd said. Of course, that wasn't the main reason she hadn't said anything. She hadn't told her mother about the incident because her mother would have been furious she'd been there in the first place. Ashby Dumping was strictly off-limits.

Melody felt awful. It might be Rudy who was killing all those animals. Suddenly she felt scared. If she was going to tell someone, she wondered if it should be Principal Fitzgibbon. Could she trust him? Rudy was a nutcase, and Melody didn't want to invoke his wrath. Maybe she could call the Sheriff anonymously.

Just then, Rudy walked by. Fitzgibbon took his gaze off Melody. His mouth dropped open and he yanked his glasses from his face.

She turned around to see Rudy waltzing by. He was wearing what looked like a black corset, skin-tight pants, and carrying some type of scepter. A long black cape cascaded behind him, trailing on the floor. As he traipsed past Fitzgibbon, he smiled wickedly. His face was painted like a vampire, with black lipstick, eyeliner and dark powder all around his eyes.

"Mr. Nobel!" Fitzgibbon cried and went running down the hall after Rudy, who took off like a bat out of Hell.

Melody went back to Logan and squeezed his arm. "See that? I'm telling you Logan, he's getting crazier," she said.

"What the...?" Logan said, without taking his eyes off Rudy, running full speed down the hall, Fitzgibbon on his tail. "He looks like a vampire!"

"Maybe he is one!" Melody said. Logan chuckled. "No, really. That was nuts."

Logan asked, "What did Fitzgibbon want with you, anyway?"

"Tell ya later. I've got to go or I'll be late."

Logan nodded and turned in the opposite direction. "Catch you later," he said. Then, suddenly he turned back around. "Melody!" he called.

She turned, walking backwards. "Yeah?"

"Uh, if you see Bevin, tell her... tell her..."

Melody stopped. "Tell her what?" she asked, feeling a shiver run up her spine.

"Tell her to call me, all right?"

"Oh...kay," she murmured, then fled down the hall to her class. She turned the corner just in time to see Van Masterson heading into the room opposite hers. He stopped and waited.

"There you are," he said, a grin spreading across his face.

Melody stopped in front of her class. "Oh, hey!" she said, nervously, fidgeting with the books in her arms. "Were you looking for me?"

Van nodded. "Just now. I almost went down to your locker to see if you were there."

"That's where I was."

Van smiled. "Are you busy tomorrow night? I mean, it's *Saturday* night — gotta do *something*," he teased.

"No!" she exclaimed quickly. Then, trying for poise, she said a little more slowly, "No, why?"

"Wanna get together? I haven't seen you around much." Melody thought of all the times she'd seen him in the halls. Of course they'd seen each other lately — he just hadn't seemed to notice her.

"I thought we could talk," Van said. He wondered if Melody had interesting witchcraft tales to impart. "You know, get to know each other."

"Sure! Maybe we can go to The Piggy and get something to eat."

"Cool. I'll meet you there."

A bell rang loudly. Melody smiled back at Van, then they both walked into their classrooms. This spell was working quicker and more easily than she'd expected. As she slid into her seat, Melody wondered if Van would have liked her anyway — even if she'd never done a love spell.

# Chapter
## ❧*21*❧

Stacey eyed the new guy. He was wearing a black shirt, jeans and a long black trench coat with the collar turned up. He was perched on the roof of the metal shed, staring down on them. He looked menacing.

"Why should we let you join our group?" Rudy demanded. He paced beneath the shed, like an animal that couldn't reach its prey.

"I told you..." Van said calmly. His eyes caught Stacey's and he smiled at her. Stacey shivered slightly. "I don't want to join *your* group. I want you to join *mine.*"

"You're crazy," Rudy barked.

"Whaddaya offerin'?" Stacey challenged. Van's blue eyes caught the moonlight like a wild animal's.

Rudy stormed over to where Stacey was sitting on the picnic bench. He got up close t her and said, "This is bullshit, Stacey. We have our *own* group, we don't need *him.*"

"What makes you so sure?" Stacey asked. She was getting tired of Rudy's crap. Besides, with Van there, she felt a little safer, like Rudy might not go off the deep end.

Stacey and Rudy looked over at Neil, who was stooped over a fire in a corroded oil barrel, gazing at its flickering flames. His hands were shoved deep inside the pockets of his jeans and, as usual, he wasn't wearing a jacket.

"Well, Neil?" Stacey asked.

Neil looked up at Van. It occurred to him that whether he'd wanted it or not, he was becoming part of a gang. Now everyone wanted to choose a leader. The pickings weren't that great. Rudy was a nutcase. At any given moment, he was likely to explode into a crazy fit of laughter or rage. He was exciting and made Neil's otherwise unbearable life interesting, but he was definitely a loose cannon.

On the other hand, no one really knew who Van Masterson was. Looking at him, perched on top of the shed like some kind of gargoyle, Neil wondered what he was after. There was something about him that wasn't quite right. But, he seemed to be more level-headed than Rudy, and he certainly had confidence.

"Dunno," Neil said shrugging, turning back to the fire.

Van looked down at Neil. "People think you don't care," he said, compassion in his voice, "The truth is, you care too much." He stood up, enjoying the befuddled look on Neil's face.

Confused, Neil looked away. "Just let him show us what he's got, Rudy," he mumbled.

Rudy scoffed. "Okay. Fine. Go on, big guy. Show us what you've got."

Van leapt from the shed, landing on his feet like an alley-cat. Caught off-guard, Rudy jumped back. Clenching his jaw, he pulled himself up to his full 6'3" height, then glared threateningly down on Van.

Van sauntered to where Stacey sat at the picnic table. He stood behind her, placing his hands on her shoulders, then gently began to massage, feeling her yield beneath his hands.

"Do you know what it means to *really* belong?" he whispered.

Stacey stiffened.

"I can offer you something you all want," Van said. "To be a part of a group that will stand by you, no matter what."

With a possessive eye, Neil watched Van rubbing Stacey's shoulders. He moved to the picnic table and sat close to her.

Trying to act indifferent, Stacey closed her eyes, allowing Van to work his magic hands across her. She liked it. It was soothing.

"I want you all to picture something," Van's voice was soft and reassuring. "You're sitting on a green bed of grass, looking up at a mountain. The sky is blue and the air is crisp, and you realize how calm and happy you are.

Stacey smiled. Next to her, Neil's clenched fists relaxed slightly.

Van continued, "You're calmer than you've ever been in your life. You're at peace."

"What's this shit?" Rudy shouted, shattering the mood.

Unfazed by the disturbance, Van continued in a soothing, yet commanding voice. "You'll see. Sit." He gestured to a seat across from Stacey.

Defiantly, Rudy stood staring at him, his arms tight at his side.

"Hey," Van said, "You're the one who said I could show you what I've got to offer. Go on, sit."

Rudy marched over to the picnic table. Reluctantly, he sat down. "Fine, but you get one shot, then I'm kicking your crazy ass back to New York, or wherever the hell you came from."

Van continued to describe a pleasant experience — a valley and a mountain range, a perfect day. After a moment, Rudy unclenched his jaw. His face began to slacken. Eyes drooping, Neil put his head on the picnic table as though he were asleep. Stacey kept her eyes shut tight, and eventually lost track of what Van was saying as his voice became a pleasant, droning buzz.

"I'm extremely powerful," Van said, when all of his subjects were relaxed. It was a simple, but strong suggestion, one of many he was implanting in the minds of the three teenagers, who were now in a vulnerable state of hypnosis. "When you see me, you'll feel good. You'll know I'm in control. I lead this Grotto, and you follow, willingly and happily."

An hour passed quickly. Rudy blinked his eyes and sighed. He was unusually calm.

Stacey smiled up at Van and said, "I feel like I just slept for a week!" She giggled and yawned.

"Is that it?" Neil asked. Watching Stacey, he yawned himself.

"What do you mean?" Van asked.

"You just get us feeling all relaxed, and that's why we should be part of your gang? I don't get it."

"You needed to be in the right frame of mind. I'm just helping you get there."

Rudy stretched, seeming uninterested. He looked around, ready to abandon the Van Masterson project and find something new to amuse him. Watching him, Stacey laughed.

"What are you laughing at?" Rudy demanded.

"Nothing," Stacey said. "You just look so calm. I've never seen you like that," and she laughed again.

# Chapter
## 22

Suddenly Stacey noticed that Van was gone. She wondered if Neil's comment had ticked him off enough to make him go. Van seemed so in control, she didn't think he'd be easily provoked or intimidated. Then she saw him reappear from behind the metal shed, carrying a black leather gym bag. He plopped it on top of the table and stepped back, as though waiting for a reaction. Stacey looked at Neil, who shrugged indifferently.

Rudy rolled his eyes. "Now what?" he said, and yawned again. "Are we gonna relax some more? Cause I think that's just another word for bor-ing!"

"No more relaxation," Van promised. "And, it's called meditation. No, now we unify our group and form our Grotto."

"Our what?" Neil asked.

"Grotto. It's like a congregation," Van answered.

"I already belong to one," Stacey said, stiffly.

Van laughed. "Admit it," he said to Stacey. "You never go to church. Besides, your church is *nothing* like this one. This is for those who seek power, not herd animals that lamely follow the pack each Sunday. And, I know you don't want to be one of the pack, do you?" he asked, looking straight into her eyes.

She shifted uncomfortably under the scrutiny of his stare. "No," he continued, "You want something more out of life, don't you? You want to get out of this place and be *a somebody.*"

Stacey's mouth dropped open. She searched Van's eyes, looking for the source of this private information. How could he know her most secret ambition? And what else did he know about her?

"Stacey, I want you to start our ritual tonight with an invocation," Van said, motioning for her to stand beside him. Reluctantly, she moved next to him, taking the piece of paper he was waving at her.

"Read this?" she asked. He nodded.

She thought about it a moment. What could it hurt? Besides, things were getting interesting. And she was feeling relaxed and a little more social after Van's strange hypnotic spell. Holding the piece of paper, she remembered how she'd read a passage from the Bible at her aunt's wedding. How different could this be?

She cleared her throat and read, "*Welcome Grotto members. We gather on Friday night, the highest night of the week, to rejoice in life. We celebrate our strengths and turn away all weaknesses. We do not waste our love on those who do not deserve it.*" Stacey paused, looking at Van. She wondered if he'd written this, knowing about her mother.

"Go on," Van encouraged. "You're doing great!"

Stacey looked back down at the paper. "*We do not waste our love on those who do not deserve it, and we do not turn the other cheek. We will take what we want from this world, enjoy it, and draw power from it.*"

She handed the paper back to Van and sat down. "Excellent!" Van praised. Stacey smiled at the rare compliment.

"Now what?" Rudy asked impatiently. But his eyes revealed genuine curiosity.

Reaching into the bag, Van began pulling items out — a black book, a large knife, an amulet with a pentagram dangling from the end.

"See man, he's just following *my* lead," Rudy complained, looking at the paraphernalia on the table.

Van turned to Rudy. His eyes narrowed and seemed to darken a shade. "Cutting the head off a chicken doesn't mean a thing. I've been doin' this a lot longer than you," he said. "And I can assure you, I've done it with the best of them."

Rudy was larger than Van, not only in height, but in muscle mass. His large black arms were bulky and well-built, the result of hours of bench-pressing weights in his basement. Working out had started as self-defense, a way to fend off his quick-tempered father. Now, Rudy liked the way he looked, and he liked the way he could intimidate.

But something about the way Van talked, the way he looked at him, made Rudy retreat. He was getting that familiar feeling in his stomach — the one he got when he was a kid and his father let Rudy know who had the power, and who didn't.

Van Masterson turned away from the picnic table and began searching the ground.

"What are you looking for?" Stacey asked, jumping up to help.

Van turned and smiled at her. A rush of excitement charged her body and she smiled back.

"I need some type of container," Van said, continuing to look around.

"Like this?" Stacey asked excitedly, holding up a rusted tomato sauce can. It was an oversized restaurant container, with vestiges of sauce encrusted on the inside.

"Perfect," he said, taking it from her.

He walked back over to the table and placed the can in front of him. Then he closed his eyes. Rudy and Neil looked at each other, locking eyes in the dark night. Shadows from the bonfire danced across their faces blending curiosity with fear.

Van looked up. Stacey was watching him, a bewitched look on her face. Van read from his black book, "*Dark forces and powers of light, show us strength and a taste for might. In this receptacle, I now will place, special offerings for your Grace."*

From the gym bag, he pulled a plastic bag containing a dark liquid. He opened the bag and dumped its contents into the can. Something solid rolled out last, and landed with a plop. A brownish-red fluid dripped from the bag.

"Heart of a wild turkey, plucked from its breast while it was still beating," Van told them.

Stacey cringed, but couldn't stop herself from watching.

Next Van pulled out a jar. He unscrewed the top and dumped a bug into the can. "A live beetle, a creature that crawls along the blackened earth," he said, then reached inside again to pull out a red bandanna.

"Fifty wings from angry hornets." Tiny iridescent wings floated down into the can as Van emptied the contents of the bandanna. He paused, watching the beetle attempt to crawl out of the rusted can, but it only slipped and fell back into the blood that coated the inside rim.

Van looked up. Excitement warmed his body. Now he would show them who was a leader. They would understand what power was, and who had it. He was — once again — in a sacred powerful Grotto. Only this time it was different. This time he was the high priest. Nothing was going to change that.

"The incantation would not be complete without this," Van said. He pulled out something small and ivory, only a few inches long.

"What's that?" Stacey asked.

"This, Stacey, is a bone," Van said. "The finger of a Christian man, who'll never point to heaven again." He tossed the digit into the can.

"Where did you get that bone?" Rudy asked, feeling upstaged. He was used to being the most outrageous person in any crowd. He peered into the can and grimaced.

"From a grave," Van said, smirking. "Where else?"

Blood rushed to Rudy's face. Once again, he pulled himself up to his full height so he could tower over Van. "What grave?" he yelled.

"You know where I got it," Van said in a level tone.

Rudy's mouth opened, then shut.

"You wanted to dig up graves that night, didn't you?" Van asked.

Stacey's eyes darted from Rudy to Van and then to Neil. She had a bad feeling.

"*You* dug up that grave?" Rudy asked.

"Well, it wasn't you, was it?" Van asked with a laugh.

Rudy shook his head. He'd spent the better part of a day in the Sheriff's office, detained and questioned for long hours and then locked up in a hot, smoky cell that smelled like piss, with a drunk who wouldn't shut up.

At first, he wondered if Stacey or Neil made up a story that it was him who'd dug up that grave. Then he heard that some old groundskeeper at the cemetery tipped off the Sheriff. Now, Rudy figured he knew who that "groundskeeper" really was.

With his new suspicions, everything in Rudy wanted to knock Van's head off. Hands clenched into fists, he started towards him. One pop and Van would be on the ground wondering if he'd ever get up again. Sweat broke out on Rudy's brow and his teeth pulled back from his lips, revealing gleaming teeth. But he couldn't do it. Something strange was going on. If it'd been anyone but Van Masterson in front of him, it would've already been over. But some inner voice prevented him from hurting Van. It was that hypnosis thing he'd done. It was like Van had put some kind of spell on them all.

Rudy and Van watched each other stubbornly, eyes locked. Then the top dog took his place. Rudy looked away.

The smile crept back onto Van's face. "Don't worry, Rudy. You're part of *real* family now. It doesn't matter what color your skin is, or whether you're big or tough enough. In this Grotto, you'll always matter and come first. We're united."

Rudy ran a hand over his face, then stepped back.

Taking a black cloth napkin from the gym bag, Van placed it over the can. "Now watch," he said, his voice rising a little.

A wind began to pick up, whipping Stacey's blonde hair about. She struggled to pin it back with a barrette.

"*Hail Satan*," Van cried into the wind. The gale lifted his long black coat, puffing it into the air like the train of a wedding dress. He closed his eyes, feeling the wind caress his face and brush his hair. This was the way to bind the group. He'd seen it work before, it would work for him now. They would be unified. Nothing would stop them then.

"*Hail Satan, Lord of the darkness,*" Van cried. "*Help us build our mighty fortress. We're your children, your soldiers of war. It is Thee, whom we fight for. Give us now our rightful powers, to vanquish enemies that cross our towers. Bind our Grotto, keep us tight. Let us shine in darkest night. So Let it Be.*"

Pages of old newspapers, paper cups and plates floated above the teenager's head as the gale increased. Above the noisy wind, Stacey laughed out loud, her hair whipping about as if it were trying to tear itself free from her head.

"Satan is my master," Van cried into the wind. "Let this be a sign we four are destined for greatness. We are destined for the power that is rightfully ours."

Giggling. There they were again. The Devil's minions. Van heard the scurrying of tiny feet. His head whipped about, searching the filthy area for the invisible, whispering little creatures. He wanted to see them. He wanted to know whom Satan had sent for his chosen one.

The wind continued to blow trash about in the air. Stacey pulled a wad of newspaper from her hair and tossed it away. Then, as suddenly as it had come, the wind stopped.

Neil clapped. "Man! That was somethin'! I've never seen anything like that before! It was like... like you made it happen. That wind!"

"Yeah," Stacey agreed, numbly. You've got my vote."

"There was supposed to be *more wind*," Van said, sounding irritated.

"Yeah, maybe next time you can flap your arms and fly around the Dump, or give us a ride to the cemetery," Rudy said sarcastically.

Van picked up the rusted can with the heart, bug, wings, and bone and flung it into the night. The can clinked on the ground, its contents spilling out.

It got quiet.

"Yeah," Van said, after a moment. "But it worked. We're a unified group now, bound to each other." He looked intently from one member to the next, his eyes stormy. "But we're missing someone," he said, looking at Stacey.

Stacey looked behind her, then at Neil and Rudy. "What do you mean?" she asked.

"We need one more person." Once we get her, it will be perfect, he promised himself.

Stacey blinked. Who was he talking about? Did he want someone else to join their gang? If there were more out there like Van, she wasn't sure she wanted to hang out with them, even if he was the most fascinating guy she'd ever met. Things were finally getting interesting in Welbourne, Kansas — but she wasn't sure yet at what price.

# Chapter
## 23

Van caught sight of them the moment he entered the diner: Ms. Popularity, Maureen Mullen, and the "guy's guy," Larry Monahan. Van strode confidently over, leaned an arm across the back of their booth, and smiled at Maureen. Eyes aloof, she looked back, then quickly down at her salad as she pushed lettuce and tomatoes around with a fork.

"Hey," Van said, a little too enthusiastically. Larry looked up, then turned his back on Van. He covered his mouth with both hands and coughed.

"Are you getting sick?" Maureen asked. She peeked up quickly, glancing at Van, then over at Larry. He held a hand up and coughed again. "No, just something in my throat," Larry said. "I'm sorry, what were you sayin', Maureen?"

Flustered, Van looked from Maureen to Larry, then scanned the diner to see if anyone saw him being rejected. At the farthest corner, he saw Melody Blackstone. She waved enthusiastically to him.

Van straightened, smoothing out his shirt. "Feel better," he said, coolly. "Gotta go." Neither Maureen nor Larry looked up as he walked away.

As Van made his way towards Melody, he wondered how he could have been interested in Maureen Mullen anyway? She was never worthy of the ritual. Never worthy of him. Just a vacant, pretty head. It'd been Melody all the time. And he'd almost overlooked her. Of course, the little witch was ideal. The perfect parallel. The perfect partner for what he had in mind.

As he approached, her smile widened. "Hi!" Melody said, motioning for him to sit down. She tried to contain her excitement.

He slid into the booth opposite her, smiling back. "I thought you were gonna stay with Maureen and Larry for a while," she said.

"Nah," Van said. "After all, I came to see *you*."

Melody blushed.

Frannie Landers walked over to the booth where Melody was sitting with that new boy, old Masterson's grandkid. Plain as day, those two were smitten.

She wondered about Mr. Masterson. No one saw much of him these days. He'd become pretty much a recluse after his wife, Missy, died, almost two years ago. That was right around the same time Leotie's husband, Erik, died, she remembered. Since then, mourning for his wife seemed to preoccupy the old man. Folks were curious about him, especially Frannie. She liked to keep her ear to the ground, her finger always on the pulse of the community. Some might think she was a bit meddlesome, but she knew she was just neighborly. Now, she wanted to find out more about the newest arrival in Welbourne.

"Hi there sweetie," she said to Melody, her lamb-chop arms poised on her wide hips. She glanced at the boy sitting opposite her in the booth. "Who's your friend?" she asked, feigning ignorance.

"Van Masterson," Melody answered, gesturing his way proudly. "He's new here," she added, sure that Frannie already knew that, and his full pedigree, too.

"Hello, Van. I've seen you around. Have you settled in all right, then?" Frannie asked.

"Yes, thanks," Van said. "Starting to feel at home, I guess."

Frannie smiled. He seemed well-mannered, she thought. At any rate, it was good to see Melody with a boy. Frannie had wondered if the girl would ever have any suitors, being that her mother raised her in the crazy fashion she did. Leotie was a good woman, hard working and honest, but witchcraft was nothing short of sinful. She loved Leotie and Melody dearly, even if their souls were doomed. She prayed for them every night.

"It's pretty busy in here today, and your mom's got her hands full," Frannie said. "So why don't I take your order."

"Can we get some apple cobbler — warm, with ice cream?" Melody asked.

"Sure can, honey. That's the best way to eat it. You just follow her lead, Van. She knows a thing or two about good home cooking," Frannie chuckled. "How's your granddaddy?" she asked. "It's too bad we haven't seen much of him lately."

"Well, you know how it's been for him," Van said. "He's just kind of holed up there in the house."

"He's got lots of friends, if he'd just reach out to them," Frannie said. She lingered, hoping she'd prompt Van to go into the details. He merely eyed her. "Well, if there's anything I can do..." Reluctantly, she turned towards the kitchen.

"So..." Melody smiled awkwardly, after Frannie left. "I wasn't sure you were ever going to talk with me again," she said, somewhat jokingly.

"What do you mean?" Van asked. He leaned back in the booth, a little perplexed. Melody seemed so vulnerable. Was she *playing* him? Was all this innocence an act? She was, after all, a witch.

"I pass you in the hall all the time and you never see me," she said, and instantly regretted it. She sounded insecure.

He noticed her, all right, Van thought. He noticed everyone. She just hadn't been that important. Until now. "Sorry if I appeared that way," he said.

"It's okay," Melody said quickly. "I don't mean to sound..."

"I guess sometimes I'm preoccupied with my problem."

"Problem?" She hoped it would be something she could help him with.

"My grandfather's not doing too well."

"Why? What's wrong with him?"

"He's sick. That's why I'm here. My father sent me to take care of him and spend time with him in case he... well, you know."

"Oh, no! What does he have?"

"Dunno. He's getting old and his health has gotten worse since I've been here."

"I'm sorry." She didn't know what to say. "I'm real close with my grandfather. I don't know what I'd do if something happened to him. Can I help?"

"I'm not sure. I've been looking into alternative medicines."

Melody brightened. "Really? Like what?"

"Herbs and things," he said casually.

"Gramps knows a lot about herbs. Maybe you and your grandfather can stop by. Our grandfathers grew up together, ya know."

Van considered this newest information. Another bond. Yes, this was definitely the perfect match.

Frannie returned with two plates piled high with apple cobbler. Steam rose from the desserts and the melting ice cream made creamy rivulets down the sides of the pastry. She placed the plates in front of her two patrons. "Well, don't just sit there smelling it!" she said with a laugh. "Dig in."

Melody shoved a forkful of apple cobbler into her mouth. "It's delicious," she said, juggling the hot pie in her mouth. Frannie wouldn't leave until people tried her food. She liked hearing the praise.

"Glad you like it. When the summer gets here, I'll be making my famous peach cobbler," she promised, with a wink.

"This is really great," Van said through his own mouthful of cobbler.

"Bring some home to your grandpa," she said to Van. "On the house, of course."

"I'm sure he'll appreciate it." He said warmly, making Frannie feel good. She hovered a moment, waiting for any tidbit of information. Then the bell above the door tinkled softly and Frannie moved away.

Melody peeked around the booth. It was Joshua Briggs, a widower who owned a large farm just outside of Welbourne. He was carrying a fistful of meadow flowers. Seating himself at the counter, he took a sticky menu from underneath the salt and pepper shakers. From the pocket of his plaid shirt, he took out a pair of reading glasses and put them on.

Leotie moved quickly from the farthest side of the diner, scooping up dirty dishes, piling them into her bucket and dropping off a check to a table of truckers. She went behind the counter and stood facing Joshua, brushing a stray hair back across her head.

"Hello, Joshua. How are you today?" Leotie asked, smiling. She paused, catching her breath, and took a pad of paper and a pen from her apron pocket.

"Afternoon," Joshua said. He smiled as he took his glasses off and looked up at her. He handed her the flowers. "Now, tell me. What's good today? I'm pretty hungry, and you know by now how much I can eat," he chuckled.

"How about the chicken fried steak?" Leotie suggested. "It comes with mashed potatoes or grits, along with white gravy."

"Sounds perfect, and I'll take the potatoes." He closed his menu and handed it to Leotie without taking his eyes off of her.

She ripped the order from her pad, put the menu back in its holder, and the pen and notepad back in her pocket. Glancing up, she caught her daughter's eye across the room. Melody looked down, pretending not to see.

She's sitting with old man Masterson's grandkid again, Leotie noticed. She watched them talking and laughing. It was obvious that Melody was very interested in him. This might very well be her first love-interest she thought. Her stomach tightened. She had a bad feeling. Instinct and intuition governed her decisions, and right now, they were telling her to beware.

Melody and Van talked on for the better part of an hour. She wanted the girls at school to see her with him. Maybe they'd be jealous of her for once.

Joshua Briggs had been eating his meal slowly. Too slow for a busy farmer with better things to do than spend the afternoon in a diner, Melody thought. Her mom chatted with him, refilling his coffee cup over and over. Maybe he was just being neighborly. Or maybe he missed his wife and wanted to talk with someone who understood. But Joshua had been a widower for as long as she could remember. And now that she thought of it, lately every time he bumped into her mother, in the hardware store or the bank, he stopped to talk.

Melody watched her mother smile and pat Joshua on the arm as he rose to leave. So much for my father's memory, she thought bitterly.

# Chapter
## 24

Melody's eyes kept fluttering shut — the text and diagrams in her Biology book too dull to keep her interest. Her head—and heart—kept switching to the subject of love.

Study hall was as quiet as a church. She looked around at the students. Most of them sat dutifully writing notes, or punching on calculators. Others, looking bored, tapped pencils, texted secretly under their desks, and stared at the ceiling, walls, or clock.

Melody kept thinking about Van. It was hard to keep her mind focused on anything else since their date at The Piggy Diner. Several times, her mother tried approaching her on the subject, but Melody avoided conversation, claiming she had outrageous amounts of homework and leaving the room. Luckily, all week her mother worked late shifts at The Piggy, so avoiding her had been easy.

She scribbled on the cover of her notebook. She didn't care what her mother thought. But that wasn't true. She wanted her to like Van, but if she didn't... Melody frowned. If she didn't, what could she do? Change the way she felt about Van?

She flipped her notebook over and began scribbling a giant heart, outlining it over and over. Something small and black scurried past her. A lab mouse on the loose? She looked at the teacher sitting up front, absorbed in the pages of *Popular Mechanics.*

Something brushed up against her. Fleshy, hairless. She shuddered, yanking her legs back and pushing her chair backward with a loud squeaking sound. Students looked up at her.

Melody's heart raced. She was certain something was scampering unnoticed on the floor.

Skittering. Melody turned her head, trying to locate the sound. The study hall teacher turned a page in his magazine. Quietly, she slid her chair forward, intently watching the floor. Suddenly, she saw it. Her mouth dropped open. A ringing sensation buzzed in her ear.

A small creature dashed across the floor, giggling madly. It was only two feet tall — if that — a small, plump hairless creature. It moved with amazing agility, pumping its arms and legs as it scurried, disappearing behind a filing cabinet.

Melody quivered. She held her breath and stared at the filing cabinet. Her eyes darted across the room. No one else had noticed the little black imp. She heard whispering, deep and low, close to her ear. She swiped at her head, looking around frantically, for the source of the sound.

Giggling again. Then, soft murmurs. From the corner of her eye, she saw a student staring at her with a baffled expression. Shaking his head, he looked back down at his book, uninterested in Melody and her problems.

Suddenly, Melody heard a voice. "When you know the stories, you have the key," the voice counseled.

# Chapter
## 25

It was Friday afternoon and the storm was relentless. The rain was coming down sideways, and the old shanty creaked and moaned as the wind beat against it. Van watched it through the window from the tiny bed at his grandfather's house. The rain struck the window like a monster trying to get in.

It reminded Van of his parents when he was growing up. He could almost hear his father's aggressive voice. "Pick it up!" he bellowed to his mother. "I said, PICK IT UP!" He was pointing to the broken Corningwear on the kitchen floor. Baked lasagna was splattered everywhere.

His father was drunk. And, about to strike his mother. A seven-year-old Van stood shivering from fright in the kitchen doorway of their Bronx apartment. His mother was crying now. On her hands and knees, she was cutting her hands as she picked up broken shards of glass.

"Please calm down, Walt," she pleaded. "I'll make ya somethin' else. Just calm down."

"Don't tell me to calm down!" he roared.

Van covered his ears and cried out, "No, dad!"

Glancing over his shoulder, his father tried to focus on the child. "Get outta here!" he screamed, waving him away. He could barely stand up. It was surprising he could even muster the ability to slap his wife, he'd get so drunk. Of course there were times when, too drunk to keep his balance, he'd simply fall like a tree to the floor, passing out for hours.

With each beating, his mother grew more dejected and distant. Then, one morning, she was gone. Disappeared. Van always wondered why she hadn't taken him. It must have been something he'd done. Why else would a mother leave her only child with a violent drunk? There was only one reason. She didn't love him. Van was bad. And now, she was dead, so there'd be no answers from her.

Someone was speaking to him again. Lying in the grungy sheets, Van smiled. The voice made him feel special, loved. "When you know the stories, you have the key," it breathed into his ear.

Van leaned over his bed, picking up a small black box from the floor. He flicked open the clasp, took out his leather-bound journal and a pen, and began to write.

Things are finally heating up. The Grotto meets again tonight. I know they wait anxiously for my direction. They admire me. I'm their Master and the Chosen One. They don't even know all the talents I have, the secrets I possess, the stories I know.
I like our church at the dumping grounds. It's so free there. We can do what we please. Sometimes we taunt the heavens to stop our madness. I think the angels cower at our enthusiasm, our lust for life. We drink, we sing, we destroy what we want. We've had

five sacrifices so far — a couple of chickens, a squirrel, a rabbit, a cat and a big old German Shepherd. We, of course, returned the cat and dog to their owners when we were done. That was Rudy's idea, and a great one, too. Melody and I have spent a lot of time together this last week. It's obvious how much she adores me. I'm waiting for her to tell me about her witchcraft. I don't know why she keeps acting like she's so nice. Does she think I'm stupid enough to be fooled by her innocent act? But I'll play this little game out until the end. Then she'll see who's the fool.

The old man is still a pain. It's easy to see why dad turned out the way he did... ignorant morons make ignorant morons. I'm still deciding what to do with him. In the meantime, his beady eyes watch everything I do. It's like we're both waiting for something to happen. And something will.

Van Masterson, April 16

# Chapter
## 26

Stacey's teeth were chattering. Her blonde hair was wet and matted to her face. Mascara dripped down her eyes; she wiped at them with cold fingers. She hated spring. Some days it was nice outside — the air fresh and clean. Other days it was cold again, as though winter tried to eke out one more day.

And then there was the rain. When she was a child, Stacey used to wish she could be someplace safe and warm to watch it rain — someplace with a fire in a fireplace and hot cocoa. It would have felt cozy to listen to thunder and watch the lightening brighten the sky for seconds at a time. But she didn't have a warm place to stay, and rain didn't make her feel cozy. It made her feel trapped.

She sat close to Neil in the metal shed with the door open, waiting for Rudy and Van to show up.

"You haven't talked to me much lately," Neil told her, watching the rain pelt the earth outside.

He wasn't watching her, but she turned to look at him. As usual, he was under-dressed for the weather, wearing only a black T-shirt and jeans, with no jacket. "Hasn't been much to say," she said.

There was a long silence. The rain continued to fall, driven fiercely to the ground by the wind. It thundered loudly. Moments later, a bolt of lightening illuminated the sky.

"Do you like him?" Neil asked.

"Who?"

"You know, Van."

She paused. "What do you mean, do I like him? You mean like a *boyfriend*?"

Neil nodded. Stacey laughed. "Are you jealous?"

Neil flashed a contemptuous look. "No. I just want to know."

Stacey considered. "Sure, I like him. He's interesting and charismatic." She smiled. "Oh, and he pays attention to me. Girls like that you know, when a guy actually pays attention to them."

He glowered, shaking his head. "You know I'm not much of a talker."

Stacey huffed. "Neil, you aren't much of anything lately."

"What's that supposed to mean?" he shot back, blood rushing to his face.

"You don't talk, you have no opinions, you don't seem to care about anyone or anything lately," she complained. The words fell out of her mouth before she could stop them. She didn't know why she was saying these things to Neil. She'd never intended to, but it was his own fault.

"Maybe I take time to make up my mind. Maybe that's why I don't talk so much or give my opinions. I take time before I decide who and what I care about," Neil fumed. "Unlike you! You just follow along with whoever tells you to follow. It could be Rudy one day or Van the next."

"What?" Stacey screeched. She backed away from Neil and then came towards him again, finger pointed towards his chest. "*I* was the one who told *you* that Rudy was bad news, remember? And as I recall, you wanted to stick by him because he was your *friend*. Who's really the follower?"

There was another uncomfortable silence. The sound of rain, wind, and heavy breathing mingled in the air.

Suddenly Neil grabbed Stacey by the shoulders and kissed her. His lips pressed firmly against hers. He moved his mouth gently against her, parting his lips slightly. Caught off guard, Stacey stiffened in the embrace. Then, she melted, her body yielding to the kiss.

When they separated, they looked at each other for a long moment. Stacey had wanted that kiss for a long time. It wasn't until recently that she'd given up on Neil completely. She was stunned into silence.

Two figures rushed the shed from the pouring rain and Stacey and Neil backed to the farthest reaches of the shelter to let them in.

"Woooeee!" Rudy cried, shaking water from his head like a dog.

"Some night, huh," Van said. He looked at Stacey, who appeared a little shaken. She had a smudge of mascara on her cheek. Van gently wiped it away with his thumb. Stacey's eyes widened and she looked at Neil, then to the ground. He followed her line of sight, a smirk spreading across his face. Neil stiffened.

"Well kids," Van said with a grin. "Ready for another night of fun?"

Rudy let out a whoop and began dancing around the small shed, bumping into everyone. Stacey lost her balance and tripped.

"Quit it, Rudy," she hissed. Neil grabbed her hand and helped her up. The shed was small and overcrowded with four people in it. "It's pitch black in here. I can't even see my hand in front of my face," she complained.

"That's why black people make better devils you know," Rudy said.

Dumfounded, Stacey said, "What?"

"If we take off all our clothes, we can run naked through the night and no one can see us."

Rudy and Van laughed uproariously. Stacey folded her arms. Once again, she was baffled by Rudy's peculiar sense of humor.

"Don't worry, Stacey," Van said. "I brought candles. He went about placing black candles all around the shed, promptly lighting them. In no time, the shed was illuminated. Flickering lights cast dancing shadows on the walls.

From a large duffel bag, Van pulled out two wool blankets. Like a concerned father, he pulled one around Neil's shoulders. "You never wear a jacket, dude," Van told him. For a moment the two locked eyes. Then, Van turned away. Neil relaxed a little, but his fist remained clenched, in a gesture that was both customary and unconscious. Van handed the other blanket to Stacey, who anxiously took it, wrapping it around herself.

"So," Rudy said clapping his hands together and blowing on them. "What are we up to tonight?"

Stacey laughed to herself. Now that the shed was softly illuminated by candles, she noticed that Rudy's eyeliner had run as well. He looked worse than she did.

Rudy was wearing makeup every day now and had tried to coerce the entire group to do the same thing. Rudy spent a whole afternoon one day after school making Neil look like a vampire. Neil liked it, but was too embarrassed to wear it to school. "I'm not as big as you are," he said to Rudy. "Guys won't hassle you about wearing lipstick, for Christ's sake."

Van was wearing his long black trench coat, his hands shoved deep in the pockets. Idly, he watched a cockroach scurry across the floor. "We have a holiday coming up," he said.

"Do we get *preeeseeents*?" Rudy asked, dancing around on tiptoes, clapping his hands.

Stacey watched him with disgust. She was certain he was going crazy. "What's the holiday?" she asked.

"Walpurgisnacht, on April 30th. It's one of our most important holidays, the grand climax of the spring equinox." Van looked at Stacey. "It's a fertility holiday."

She blushed.

"Yeah? Well what about the presents?" Rudy asked.

Van laughed. "'*Strive ever for more, for conquest is never done.*' That's from the *Black Book of Satan.* You can have whatever you want, Rudy, you just have to know how to get it." He paused, folding his arms across his chest, then added, "On April 30th, we're going to open the gates to Hell."

The shed was suddenly quiet. Thunder rumbled in the distance.

"What?" asked Neil.

"No more chicken sacrifices and petty rituals. This will be our finest moment." Van crouched in a corner of the shed, his features distorted in the candle-light. Shadows hung beneath his eyes making his face appear sunken and hollow. "When we open a portal to Hell, we call on all the powers of Satan's minions. We can have all the riches, all the wealth, all the power and respect we want. We can be famous if we want," he said looking straight at Stacey.

"People will worship us. All we have to do is let Satan know that we are his soldiers. '*Come as a reaper, for thus you will sow.*'"

"How do we do all that?" Neil asked.

Van patted the top of the book he was holding. "With all of us working together, we can do it. I know how." He looked straight at Stacey, "You'd never have to go home again. Why would you have to, if you had all the money you wanted?"

Stacey's head tingled with excitement. She saw herself in Los Angeles, driving a bright red convertible. She pictured the apartment she'd have, everything expensive and new.

Van turned to Rudy and said, "No one would disrespect you again. All the people that ever did you wrong would know it. They'd piss their pants, just wishing that you'd be their friend."

Rudy laughed loudly. "Man, you know how to say it."

"And Neil would never feel lonely again," Van continued, moving on to the next member of the group. "Everyone would want to be near you."

Neil was visibly rattled. He shook his head, his black hair falling into his face. "What are you, the goddamn Wizard of Oz?" he asked snidely. "A brain for the scarecrow, a heart for the tinman, courage for the lion. Just click my heels and whoops... we're not in Kansas anymore!"

Stacey laughed.

"I'm going to introduce someone else to the Grotto," Van went on, ignoring the sarcasm. "It's important. We need her."

Stacey wasn't sure she liked the idea of another girl joining them. "Who?" she demanded, hands on her hips.

"Melody Blackstone."

"What!" Stacey cried. "Why her? She's weird. She practices witchcraft, or something like that."

Van laughed out loud. "Stacey," he reminded her, "we worship Satan!"

Stacey looked around the room. No one laughed. Her mouth opened, and hung like that for a moment as she wondered what to say. "I... I don't worship Satan," she stuttered. "I go to church, remember? My parents are both Baptist. *I'm* Baptist."

"Really?" Van asked. The blood rushed to his face, causing a pulsating ringing in his ears. He stood up and moved closer to her. "Then what have you been doing with us all this time — while we sacrificed animals, did our rituals, drank blood, and painted our bodies?" He paused, watching her. "Going to church?" He laughed.

Stacey was stunned. The color drained from her face. She glanced at Neil, but she should have known better than to expect him to come to her rescue. As usual, he stood quietly watching, offering no opinion, no comment, not making a move to defend her.

"I thought we were just having fun," Stacey said weakly, her voice trailing off.

"Oh, we are," Van said. "And we're going to have more fun. You just have to decide if you're on board or not." His face turned serious. His eyes were small and tight and his mouth turned down in a scowl. Then, in the cold, dimly-lit shed, his eyes began to glow a soft orange. At least it looked that way to Stacey. Suddenly, she was frightened. For the first time since she'd started hanging around with these guys, she realized how vulnerable she was, how alone.

But where could she go? Home? That wasn't an option. Home was a hostile environment. At least in the Grotto, if she pledged commitment, she would belong someplace, maybe even be protected.

Van waited for her. She could hear his heavy breathing and the whistling sound it made at the back of his throat. The hair on the back of her neck stood up.

"I'm on board," she said, her mouth trembling. "I guess I didn't understand."

"Stacey's cool," Rudy said. "She's one of us."

Van nodded at Rudy. "What about Melody?"

"Bring her," Stacey said trying to sound convincing. "It'd be good to have another girl as a member of the group."

"Who said I wanted her as a member?" Van said coldly. Stacey shivered.

Van handed several pieces of paper to the three teenagers. "We need to collect these things. You've got one week. It may take some work, but I'm sure you won't disappoint me."

# Chapter
## ❧27❧

The porch screen door banged loudly. Melody glanced up at the old grandfather clock from where she sat curled up on the couch, her cat Willow in her lap. It was almost 9 p.m. That was either her mother, or the storm had ripped the latch off the door again.

Snoring loudly in his old recliner, Earl woke suddenly as the door opened and a gust of chilly wind blew in. Leotie entered, drenched.

Melody got up, kicking the blanket off from around her, along with the cat and the book she'd been holding. All day she couldn't shake the horrible image of the little black imp she'd seen in study hall. Having time to rationalize, at this point she was convinced she'd fallen asleep and dreamed the whole thing. Either that or she'd gone into a trance. Her body, conditioned to undergoing the experience, might have done it automatically. She wished she really knew why this was happening to her and how to make it stop.

"You're soaked," Melody said, shaking her thoughts away and helping her mother with two bags of kitchen leftovers from the diner. "Why are you so wet?"

Leotie released the bags to Melody. "Well, it's raining outside," she pointed out, somewhat sarcastically.

A clap of thunder rocked the house. A moment later lightening brightened all the windows.

"I know *that*," Melody said. "But you were parked right outside The Piggy Diner. The truck was only two steps away. You look like you walked home in the rain!"

"I almost had to," Leotie said. Her wet umbrella fell to the floor as she pulled her dripping wet coat off. It was smeared with mud.

Melody was alarmed by the look on her mother's face. "What do you mean?"

"Someone slashed my tires!" she said angrily.

Melody ran to the kitchen for a dish towel and pushed it in her mother's hands. Leotie's hair hung in wet clumps around her face.

"It's been a horrible day," she said, her voice just above a whisper.

"Know who did it?" Earl asked, a worried look on his face.

Leotie shook her head. "The rain was coming down hard. I went out to the truck, but when I tried to drive away, I realized something was wrong. I got out and saw that all four tires were slashed! But that wasn't the worst of it. Just as I started to go back to the diner to call you, Earl, four teenagers suddenly appeared and started screaming at me. They threw something at me, and I was so scared I fell.

"I couldn't understand what they were saying. The rain was pelting my head. I was sitting there in a puddle of mud with the tires on my truck slashed with four kids screaming at the top of their lungs. When I realized what they'd thrown at me, I started screaming, too. That shut them up pretty fast because," she gave a weak little laugh, "well, you know how loud I can scream."

"What did they throw?" Melody asked.

"A dead chicken," Leotie answered with a shiver of repulsion. "Its head was cut off and it was caked with blood."

Melody gasped. Convinced she knew who did it, guilt welled up in her chest. She dropped her eyes.

"That's terrible!" Earl cried, furious. "What's happening to this town? What kind of a kid does a thing like that? What kind of parents do they have?" His voice rose with each question, until he was bellowing.

Leotie blew her nose. She took off her shoes and began toweling her wet hair.

"Did you call the Sheriff?" Earl wanted to know.

"No, not yet."

"Well, how'd you get home? Don't tell me you walked!"

She hesitated. "One of my customers brought me home. He's a real nice man, Joshua Briggs. You know him, don't you Melody?"

Melody nodded, turning away. She had a good idea why Joshua Briggs was being so nice to her mom, while the rest of the town found fault with her.

"Actually, he was the last person to leave the diner. He left about the same time I did," she told them. "He was halfway to his car when he heard me screaming, and came running back. Lucky he was there."

Melody went back into the kitchen, filled the tea kettle with water, and put it on the stove. While she was gone, Leotie turned to Earl, her expression grim. "That chicken was mangled," she said in a low voice.

"They ought to find those crazy kids and lock 'em up," Earl said angrily.

"I don't think it was those kids that killed the chicken."

"What do you mean?"

"At first I couldn't understand what they were screaming at me. Everything was happening at once, and it was confusing. But then I listened to what they were saying. *Someone else* had killed it and they thought it was *me*."

"Why you?" Melody asked, from the kitchen doorway.

"It's not just me, Melody," she told her daughter gently. "They think all *three* of us do things like that. They were shrieking things like 'filthy family of witches!' and 'Your evil witchcraft won't work on us!'

"I'm used to how ignorant some people can be," she continued. "Some folks have blamed me when not enough rain falls for the crops in the summer, or when there's damaging hail in the winter, as if I have something to do with the weather. But this is different. I'm hearing about animal sacrifices and pentagrams showing up on tombstones, and this town is accusing us. At the diner, some folks won't let me serve them. They're afraid I'm going to poison their food or put toad parts in their omelets."

"This town never did understand Wicca," Earl grumbled. He paced the living room floor, frowning with worry.

"Mom," Melody said cautiously. "I have something to tell you."

"Go on."

"I think I know who's been doing those animal sacrifices."

Leotie gave her daughter a level stare. Melody swallowed hard, then explained what she'd seen at Ashby Dumping — how Rudy had held the chicken up, slit its throat and drank its blood. She told her mother how she'd seen Rudy around school wearing black make-up and outrageous clothing lately. Her mother and grandfather were quiet for a moment. Earl had his arms wrapped tightly around his chest.

"What on earth were you doing at Ashby Dumping? And why didn't you tell us this before?" Leotie demanded.

Melody opened her mouth to tell about her trances and the strange visions she'd been having, why she'd gone to the cemetery and how she'd ended up at Ashby Dumping. She wanted to talk to her mother the way they *used* to talk. Then she could explain why she didn't want to "tell" on Rudy, how she felt a mixture of fear, plus not wanting to be even more "different" by having a big mouth. But she couldn't seem to find a place to start, so she shrugged, looking helplessly at her grandfather.

Earl had a funny expression on his face. They agreed that in the morning Earl would drive Melody and her mother to the Sheriff's office to report what Melody had seen, as well as the tire-slashing incident.

Suddenly there were several knocks at the door.

"Now who would that be, on a night like this?" Earl grumbled.

"I don't know," Leotie said rising from the couch. She looked at Melody. "Are you expecting anyone?"

"No! Maybe you shouldn't answer it!"

"Good grief, Melody. No one is going to intimidate me, especially not in my own home." She made her way to the side porch door, turned the light on, and peered out. "Well, I'll be," she murmured.

"Who is it?" Melody asked, standing nervously behind her.

"A ghost from the past," she said, opening the door wide.

The rain poured in sideways as a wrinkled, shabbily dressed man, about the age of Melody's grandfather, stood in the doorway. He was holding on tightly to a large black umbrella, his other hand shoved deep in the pocket of his overalls.

"Come in," Leotie encouraged.

He shuffled slowly across the threshold, dripping water and tracking in mud. Leotie took his wet overcoat and umbrella. "You have good timing. We were just about to enjoy a pot of tea," she told the old man.

"That'd be real fine, Leotie," the old man replied, his voice croaking.

Earl moved slowly into the kitchen. He had a bad hip and it took him longer to walk from room to room when the weather was stormy and the humidity was high.

Seeing the visitor in his kitchen, he stopped short, his face clouded with a peculiar expression of mixed emotions. "Well," he said, clearing his voice. "Look what the storm washed to my door." He extended a hand to the old man.

"Melody, you remember Van Masterson," Leotie said, turning to her daughter. "He's an old friend of your Grandpa's."

"Course," Melody stammered. It'd been several years since she'd last seen him. She stared at him curiously, seeing him differently now because he was Van's grandfather.

The old man smiled. "You must know my grandson," he said.

"I do! He's real nice," she chirped.

"What brings you out here on such a terrible night, Van?" Leotie asked, handing him a cup of tea. She motioned for him to sit at the table.

"I hope I'm not inconveniencing anyone," Van said. "I'm sure you folks weren't expecting company, so maybe I better..."

"No, no," Earl said. The two older men stared at each other for a moment. There was a quiet hesitation. "Stay."

"Would have called, but..." Van looked up at Earl, his eyes narrowing, "No phone. Haven't had one for awhile now."

"Yup," Earl said. "Can understand that. Sometimes it's nothing but a nuisance."

The two men nodded. Van sipped his tea. Leotie returned to the table with cream and sugar, and two more cups of tea for herself and Earl. "Even so, you ought to have a phone, Van," she scolded. "You never know when you might have an emergency." She looked up at Melody. "Maybe you'd better go upstairs, hon," she suggested.

Melody had been looking carefully at old Mr. Masterson. He didn't look sick, she decided, thinking of what his grandson had told her. But she noticed that his hand shook when he brought the cup of tea to his mouth. She wondered what was wrong with him and what prompted a visit, especially on such a stormy night, to an old friend he hadn't seen in years. Maybe Van had taken her suggestion and told his grandfather to come by for some advice on healing herbs.

Melody took a few steps toward the front hall, then turned around. "Mr. Masterson?"

The old man looked up from his tea, squinting at her.

"How's your health?" she asked.

The old man blinked. "Fit as a fiddle, young lady," he said, and chuckled.

Melody was puzzled. She opened her mouth slightly as if to ask something else, then closed it. Maybe he didn't want to discuss his illness with a teenager, she thought. After a pause she asked, "Is your grandson okay? I mean, he wasn't at school today."

The old man paused. "Well, I'm sure he'll be back in school on Monday," he said, finally.

Melody watched him for a moment. "Well, I guess I'll go to my room now," she said quietly. "Nice seeing you again."

# Chapter
## 28

After Melody left, old man Masterson took out a handkerchief and pressed it to his mouth. He rubbed his face and eyelids.

"Van," Earl said quietly. "What's going on? It's been two years and..."

"I'm sorry," Van said slowly. He was quiet for a moment. "So many times I wanted to stop by. I haven't seen much of anyone lately."

"When Erik died," Earl said, then closed his eyes, the pain of his son's death still fresh. "Know Missy passed and all, but then Erik... and we ain't seen ya since."

Van nodded. "You're kind to be so neighborly after such a long spell."

Earl sipped his tea and waited for Van to explain the reason for his visit.

"It's my grandson," the old man said finally. He held his teacup in both hands, letting the steam rise into his withered face. "My son sent him to me a month or so back. Folks think we old people get lonely. Maybe there's some truth there. But I finished raising my family, done with that a long time ago. I didn't want the responsibility. But, well, what could I do?"

Leotie and Earl nodded. They sat quietly drinking their tea, patiently giving the conversation over to Van.

"There's some things I don't understand and I don't know who else to talk to. Thought about calling his father, but he ain't no use. He's been lettin' that boy do as he pleases for years now. The boy's mother ran off when he was just small."

"What's the problem with your grandson?" Earl asked. He got up to get oatmeal cookies from the bread box. He couldn't sit at the table for too long without something sweet to eat.

"Well, for one thing, he's been missing for a couple of days."

"Oh no!" Leotie exclaimed, alarmed. "You have to call the Sheriff."

Van shook his head. "He'll be back. He's done this kind of thing before."

"That's awful!" Leotie said. "You must be so worried. If that were Melody, I don't know what I'd do."

Van said, "Ma'am, I reckon your Melody wouldn't do something like that, because she weren't raised to do it."

Leotie sighed, feeling pity for the old man.

"You done a good job with her, but my grandson..." Van shook his head. "I found some things in his room. Mind you, I weren't looking for nothing, but sometimes I gotta get in there. He's been living in my old storage room, ya see. I keep things in there, stuff I don't need too often. I've been havin' some trouble with my memory lately, and I just couldn't figure out for the life of me when Missy's birthday was. I've got a box of old birthday cards and such — thought I might find the answer there. Then I came across this..."

He placed a chain with a pentagram dangling from it on the table.

"You folks know what this is, right?" Van asked. He looked hopeful, not accusatory. Leotie reached across the table and took the pentagram in her hands.

"Yes, we know what it is," she said. "It's a pentagram."

"Can you tell me about it?" Van asked.

"It's a commonly misunderstood symbol," she replied. "People often mistake it for something demonic. As Wiccans, we use the pentagram in many of our rituals. It's an ancient symbol representing unity." Leotie paused, watching Van carefully. "But that doesn't help you, does it?" she asked.

"Wish it did," Van said. "I don't think my grandson is wearing this thin' 'cause he thinks it means unity."

"Maybe not," she said, looking troubled. She glanced at Earl, her eyes imploring him to offer advice to his friend.

Earl cleared his voice. "Now, Van," he said, "What exactly do you think is the problem with your grandson?"

"Damned if I know," Van said. He got up and moved to his tattered, wet raincoat draped over the countertop. He pulled a brown paper bag from the pocket and brought it over to the table. "What do you reckon all this is?" he asked placing several objects in front of them.

Leotie jerked back. In a canning jar was what appeared to be a small animal heart, floating in clear liquid, probably formaldehyde. Next to it was a black book. Leotie picked it up, read the cover, and promptly dropped it back onto the table. "Your grandson may be involved in a Satanic cult, Van," she said coolly.

Earl glanced over at the book. The *Black Book of Satan* was etched in white letters on the cover.

Van rubbed his eyelids again. He hadn't slept in quite a while, and the deprivation was making him jittery.

Leotie leaned in close to the old man, putting her hand on top of his. "Have you tried talking with him? I know kids can be difficult at this age," she said, thinking of the rift that had grown between herself and her own daughter. "But maybe he's in some kind of trouble. If you try to find out why he leaves, and why he's bringing items like these into your home, maybe you could help him."

"I don't know 'bout these things," Van said quietly. He glanced at Earl and the two exchanged a knowing look. "I'll be honest, I ain't that good with kids, never have been. Frankly, we didn't do so good with Walt. As soon as he was old enough, he left and never came back. Now he's gone and messed up his own son. Guess these things just keep goin'.

"Nah, I don't know what to say to that boy. When I saw these things," he held up the book and the necklace, "well, I thought that maybe you could help. I've known you for a long time, Earl," he said, his glassy blue eyes holding his old friend's gaze.

"I know you ain't a church-goin' man. And, course I know you're a witch. But I know you're good folks."

Earl nodded. "We go back, Van. There's history there."

"Van, I suggest you call the Sheriff right away," Leotie urged. "Even if his disappearing act is routine, your grandson could be in serious danger."

"No, no," Van said shaking his head. "No Sheriff. Not now. Maybe he's just dabblin', doin' spells, just bein' a kid an' all." Again, he held Earl's gaze. The two spoke of the past without uttering a word. "In the meantime, I'm askin' ya kindly not to involve the law. This is still a family matter."

Despite Leotie's and Earl's repeated urgings that he call the Sheriff, Masterson left without making any promises. There was little more they could say when the old man put on his overcoat and headed back out into the stormy night.

Standing on the porch, Van turned to Earl, his face haggard. "I... I... come to tell ya somethin' else, Earl," he said. He hesitated, the wind whipping at his back. "I want you to know I'm sorry."

"For what?" Earl asked, thinking Van must mean how he'd let their friendship lapse after his son died.

"I always thought that if I walked in the path of God, went to church, well, that was all I had to do. I've tried to be a man of God, Earl. A man of God," he repeated, almost to himself. "I always thought I knew what was right and what was wrong."

"Not sure I'm followin' what you're sayin', Van," Earl said, feeling uneasy. He had the feeling there was more to Van's story than he knew.

Suddenly Van reached forward, his wet hands clutching Earl's like a life-raft. "I was wrong. I shoulda done different. I'm sorry," he said, and quickly turned, charging back into the tempest.

# Chapter
## ☙29☙

That night, for the first time since his death, Melody dreamed about her father in a way that she knew it was divination. She was in a smoky, dark place. People talked and mingled. There was the hustle and bustle of waitresses moving about, the strong smell of grilled steaks and other foods cooking.

Looking around, Melody was stunned. She was at a tavern about fifteen miles from town. It was *The Last Drop Pub & Grill*, the place where her father had been killed.

Her father sat across from her in a booth, a plate of fried chicken in front of him. He smiled at her. "Daddy?" she said, hopefully.

"Eat up, sweetie. It's gonna get cold," he said, winking. Melody looked down to see a steaming hot plate of spaghetti and meatballs smothered in sauce, her favorite meal. She looked back up at her dad. He looked content as he watched her, a glow on his face.

"Dad, you need to help me," she said. "No one else would understand."

"That's not true, pumpkin, you know that," he said. His eyes twinkled as he spoke. "Your mom and grandpa love you more than you could ever know. You're not giving them a chance."

Melody lowered her eyes. "I'm just so... so..."

"Angry?"

"I want to blame someone."

"It was an accident," Melody. "There's no one to blame, and certainly not your mother, who loves you so much. Don't keep punishing her for something she wasn't responsible for."

Melody's lower lip trembled. She nodded. "Dad... why am I having these visions? What's going on?"

Her father leaned forward, and suddenly she smelled lavender, the scent of the after-shave he used to wear. She remembered a flower lore, how lavender was used by witches to work magic against unresolved guilt. She was suddenly so lonely for him, she could have cried.

"Melody, you know the Wiccan rede, '*Mind the threefold law you should, three times bad and three times good.*'"

"Of course I know it. But what have I done?" she asked, even as she thought of the spells she'd cast.

"It isn't just your spells, Melody," he said, his face somber. "It's what you ask for in your heart. You have brought forth the very thing you sought."

"Little black imps? I never wanted this. I never even wanted the gift of second sight," she cried, dismayed.

Melody turned away, looking around the room. In a darkened corner of the smoky room, she spied an old man sitting in a booth. She squinted, trying to see him better, certain she recognized him. He turned his head and she saw it was the senior Van Masterson. What was he doing here, she wondered?

She looked back to her father. He looked angelic. "*Bide the Wiccan Laws we must, in Perfect Love and Perfect Trust. Perfect power holds no might, only love we seek is right. See not with your eyes the visions, use your heart and intuition. Grown from greed, pain and fright, be not fooled to think it sight. And when the demon comes for you, know your faith and keep it true.*"

Melody opened her eyes, the dream still vivid. She got herself ready for the day and waited for her mother in her grandfather's ancient pick-up truck. It was early in the morning, so she started the car and put the heater on.

"Where's mom?" she asked, when her grandfather, clad in his best dark blue overalls, climbed into the truck.

"Not comin'," he said. He got behind the wheel of the truck, put it in gear, and started to drive down the bumpy dirt road. In between bumps, he tried catching sips of hot coffee from his cup.

Melody yawned and closed her eyes. Maybe she could get a few more winks of sleep.

"Melody?" Earl said finally.

She opened one eye. "Hmmm?"

"That new boy you've been hanging around with lately... Van Masterson..."

Melody opened her eyes and sat up. "Yeah?"

"How much do you know about that boy?"

"I don't know, not much, I guess. Why does everyone ask me that question? He seems nice, Gramps." Her heart began to sink, as she sensed some type of limitation coming on. "*Really.*"

As Earl took another sip of coffee, he hit a bump. Coffee splashed his mouth, neck and shirt. Melody handed him napkins from the glove compartment. "Darn," he grumbled, taking his eyes from the road to mop at his overalls and T-shirt. "Not sure I want ya hanging 'round him," he told her.

"What! *Why not?*"

He looked over at his granddaughter, worry in his eyes. "Think he might be involved in some bad things..."

"I don't believe this! I finally meet a boy I like, who likes *me*, and now you and mom decide you don't want me to see him again? You don't even know him! How do you know what he's involved in?"

"Now girl..." Earl began, "I don't think ya understand..."

"You're right! I don't!" Melody crossed her arms in front of her chest, her chin thrust forward. She was furious.

"Last night, his grandfather told us he's been missing for a few days," he explained, trying to keep his voice and temper even. "He ain't come home, or even called. His grandfather don't have any idea where he is or what he's been up to. But it can't be good."

Raising her eyebrows, Melody looked over at her grandfather. She could see how concerned he was, and that worried her. She couldn't imagine what old man Masterson had said to him last night.

"Not the first time he's done this," Earl continued.

Melody stared at the road, saying nothing.

"That love spell..." Earl said, picking his words carefully. "Think I know who that was for. Listen, pumpkin, I have a lifetime's experience on these matters. Too much, tell the truth. Think ya understand those things, that you can handle them, but... everythin' has a price.

"The spells we do, the rituals, it's ain't for gettin' things we want all the time. Most important things in life are won on their own merits, without the aid of magic. More ya do on your own, more ya work for the things ya want, more you'll appreciate magic. But, ya have a long way to go. Lots a growing to do."

Melody didn't respond. The truck moved off the dirt road onto the paved highway. She looked out the window at the long flat road ahead, wishing she was someplace far away. She was sure that the reason Gramps had taken her alone was to have a private chat with her and try to convince her not to see Van anymore. She knew her mother thought Gramps would be more convincing.

She thought about the things Gramps had said, and wondered where Van stayed when he left his grandfather's house. Where did he sleep and why would he leave?

She'd heard old Masterson was getting weird, that he'd turned into a recluse who never left the house. Van said his grandfather was strict, but maybe he was really a tyrant, and Van didn't want his friends to know how bad things were at home for him. The more she thought about it, the more she wondered why she should trust the word of some old hermit, who suddenly showed up at their house with bad things to say about his own grandson.

She decided she'd give Van the benefit of the doubt. Maybe there was a reasonable explanation for everything her grandfather said.

"Gramps," she asked as they pulled into the parking lot at the Sheriff's office. "Why'd Mr. Masterson stop coming around to see you? Was it because his wife died?"

He parked the truck and shut off the engine, turning to face Melody. "Dunno. It wasn't after Missy died, though. No, he was real sad, but he'd still come around to talk." He thought a moment. "It was later, after Erik died that we stopped seeing him." He sighed deeply. "Maybe it was just too much for the old geezer. He thought of Erik as his own son. Walt, his boy, didn't turn out that great. Guess he thought Erik was the son he shoulda had."

At the Sheriff's office, Earl and Melody sat restlessly in cracked leather chairs, waiting for Sheriff William Larkin. The office was small, dominated by the Sheriff's large desk, cluttered with paper. Almost buried under the paper pile was a small laptop.

Sheriff Larkin was originally from a small town near Houston, Texas. An outsider with an insider's mentality, the Sheriff understood the town, the politics, the local mode of thought. He'd made an effort to get to know most everyone in Welbourne, and to understand what their individual stories were. He was a kind man with a no-bull attitude.

The door swung open and the Sheriff entered, wearing a cowboy hat. He tipped it slightly in their direction and settled himself heavily behind his desk, moving his chair back a bit to make room for his legs.

"Mornin' folks," he said politely, opening a drawer and pulling out a manila folder. "Gimmee just a minute here." He removed some papers from the file and quickly scanned them. Finally, he looked up at Earl and Melody.

"Mr. Blackstone, thank you for coming today," he said. His Midwestern twang held a slight southern drawl. "Sorry you had to wait so long."

Earl nodded. "As I was tellin' the Deputy, Leotie don't know who those teenagers were that slashed her tires. Raining pretty hard last night, but maybe she could tell ya what they were wearing..."

The Sheriff shook his head. "There's no need," he said cutting him off. "We have some idea who they were."

Earl and Melody looked at one another with surprise and relief.

"In any event, proving that the same kids who harassed Mrs. Blackstone also slashed your tires won't be easy."

"Don't think I understand."

"Sir," Sheriff Larkin said, leaning back in his chair and folding his arms across his chest, "your coming in here today saved us a trip out to your farm."

Earl stared blankly at the Sheriff. Why would he want to come to Blackstone farm?

"You see, several complaints have been filed against your family..." he shifted his gaze over to Melody, "...regarding the mutilation and killings of pets and barn animals." The Sheriff held up the file he'd been looking through. "Based on what you've told us, I reckon the kids that tossed the dead chicken at Mrs. Blackstone last night might belong to one of the folks that complained about ya'll."

"That's just darn foolish!" Earl said, his sun-weathered face narrowing in anger. "We came here today on account of my daughter-in-law bein' harassed. She was terrified and didn't deserve it. Expect you to find who did it and put them on notice that this kind of thing can't happen again. As to those reports, our family would never kill *any* animals, never mind mutilate them! What do you think we *are*?"

The room was silent. Sheriff Larkin tapped a pencil on his desk, watching Earl and Melody closely.

"'Sides," Earl said, sitting up straighter in his chair, "my granddaughter told your Deputy who did those terrible acts," he argued. "She *saw* them at Ashby Dumping."

The Sheriff looked at Melody. Her mouth was tight, her expression the same as her grandfather's. "Yes, sir, so you both say," the Sheriff said. "But I have to be honest. It looks like your granddaughter might have concocted that story to take the blame off her."

"Are you nuts?" Melody screeched, rising from her chair.

"Hush," Earl said, flashing his granddaughter a look warning her to remain dignified. Melody sat back down.

"Mr. Blackstone, let me assure you that we will investigate all angles on this one. We'll get to the bottom of it, no matter what. So, if your granddaughter is telling the truth, she has nothing to worry about." Sheriff Larkin went back to tapping his pencil.

"What now?" Earl asked, trying to sound calm.

"Go home. We'll let you know when we find something, or when we want to talk to you again."

# Chapter
## 30

Melody heard the snickering at the back of class, caught the whispers as she walked down corridors, and read the note taped on her locker door, warning her to stop sacrificing animals and leave town.

Logan and Bevin tried consoling her, but they were ridiculed too — after all, they were her friends. Logan had lost any hope of dating the popular girl in his History class. He'd given up shaving — his goatee was growing back — and he'd started wearing concert T-shirts again. Well, Melody thought, at least he was showing an interest in Bevin.

She went home alone, straight to the altar. She prayed to the Earth Mother, offered flowers and herbs, and then ate freshly baked bread in her honor. She lit incense and sang, but nothing seemed to lift her spirits. Everything in her life, it seemed, was unraveling.

Midweek, she finally saw Van Masterson in school. He'd been missing for almost a week. She'd heard that some kids had seen him around town the previous Friday — although he hadn't come to school and hadn't, according to Gramps, stayed at his grandfather's house. Melody wondered where he'd gone and what he'd been doing all that time.

Now, he was standing by her locker. Dressed in his usual black attire, he watched the students pass by, waiting patiently for Melody. Seeing him, her heart raced. She felt like running into his arms. "Where have you *been*?"

"I'll tell you later," Van said. Eyes sparkling, he bent slowly to kiss her. Caught off guard, she almost turned away. Their lips touched, and a warmth flooded her, weakening her completely.

When he pulled away, every part of her body tingled. She suddenly didn't care anymore what anyone thought, not the kids at school, not the Sheriff, not even Gramps.

Van said, "You know where Ashby Dumping is?"

She nodded.

"Can you meet me there after school?" he asked.

She choked down the automatic "no" that came to her mind. "All right," she said.

"Great. I have so much to tell you."

Van winked and left. Melody didn't know if he was going to class, or leaving again.

In Biology, the beautiful Maureen Mullen sat flipping her long blonde hair and passing notes to her friends. Melody was quiet, trying to be unnoticed. As the class went on, she took notes, watched the clock, and tried to count how many times Maureen flipped her hair.

Suddenly Maureen put her head down on her desk. Several students looked over trying to figure out what was going on. She turned sideways in her desk, cradling her head in her hands. Headache again, thought Melody. Without thinking, she reached into her backpack, groping for her herbal headache remedy. Maureen looked over at her. "What are you staring at?" she demanded.

Melody let go of the packet. "Nothing," she said. "It just looks like you have a splitting headache."

Maureen huffed. "Is that supposed to make me think you're psychic?" She put trembling hands up to her temples and began rubbing. Her perfectly made-up face was a ghastly white.

Hands on her hips, Ms. Harell approached the two girls whispering in her class. Her pitiless eyes focused on Melody.

Maureen, hands still on her head, asked to be excused to the nurses' office. Ms. Harell nodded. "Go along, Maureen," she said still glaring at Melody. "As for you, Ms. Blackstone, I'm tired of warning you. I think you'd better take a trip to the Principal's office," she said coldly.

Melody sat on the long bench outside the Principal's office. She examined her fingernails and sketched on her notebook. No matter what, she wouldn't let this get to her. She was beginning to say that to herself all the time, over and over, like a mantra. Besides, she could think of Van now and be happy. She could think of kissing him and the way it made her feel. It took her someplace else.

A cold hand on her shoulder. Melody jumped.

"Sorry. I didn't mean to frighten you," said Principal Fitzgibbon. "Come on in."

It was the first time Melody had been sent to the office, and she wondered just what she was in for. But she saw immediately that Fitzgibbon was being surprisingly kind. He gestured to the seat opposite his desk, inviting her to sit, and offered her some hard candy from a bowl. She declined. He took one himself, leaned back in his chair and cradled his arms behind his head.

"So, want to tell me what happened?" he asked.

Seeing him so relaxed, she began to feel safe. Melody sat back in her chair, took a deep breath, then explained what had happened in class, even about the herbal headache remedy she'd thought of giving Maureen.

"You know, you're not supposed to have that on school grounds," he said. "It's against regulations."

She blushed. "I didn't know."

"Of course not. Just don't bring it in tomorrow, okay?" He smiled warmly at her.

"I won't," she said.

Fitzgibbon nodded. "That's all," he said. "You can go now."

Melody looked at the door. She didn't want to go back to Ms. Harell's class. The kids would look at her. She'd be an open target, and she couldn't take it any more.

"Is there a problem?" Fitzgibbon asked. He took another sour ball from the bowl on his desk and again offered one to Melody. This time she took one.

"I didn't mean to cause any problem," she said. "I've just been having a terrible week."

"I know," Fitzgibbon said. He leaned back again, relaxing in his swivel chair, putting his hands on top of his bald head. Melody could hear the soft sucking noises he was making on the candy, like a small child. She'd never spent much time around Principal Fitzgibbon. He'd occasionally spoken to her in the hallway, and once he'd reprimanded her. She knew his reputation with the students — severe, punitive, and somewhat dull. But that wasn't the man who sat in front of her. He seemed approachable and warm. She remembered how he'd put an arm around a lost and emotionally wounded Neil Carey.

"How did you know?" Melody asked.

"I know what's happening in my school, Ms. Blackstone. I try to understand my students, even if I can't always interact with them as often as I'd like."

Melody leaned forward in her chair. "Then you know what they think — that I did those terrible things to those animals?"

"I've heard," Principal Fitzgibbon said without flinching. He began munching on the candy in his mouth.

"I didn't do it," she said, speaking softly and with emotion. Suddenly, she wanted someone to understand.

"I know you didn't," he said evenly.

"How do you know?"

"I'm fairly certain I know who's responsible."

"You know? Then why don't you tell the Sheriff? He thinks I did it. Me and my family!"

"That's not necessarily true. And I've spoken to the Sheriff about this on several occasions."

"So why does everyone still think I did it?"

"Melody," Principal Fitzgibbon said, pulling his chair closer to the desk, "This is primarily a fundamentalist Christian community. Religious groups like Men for Christ, and The Christian Women's Organization do not like people like you and your family. They have tremendous power in this town, and by their standards, you are heathens. If you don't worship their God, then you must be worshipping something far more sinister — like the Devil. You can't expect them to understand people like you. The best you can hope for is that, with luck, they might tolerate you.

"When something pernicious happens in town, when they see pentagrams on tombstones, they'll assume you had something to do with it. You are, after all, witches."

Fitzgibbon leaned back in his chair again and eyed Melody. "'Course, you never heard that from me."

Melody didn't know whether what he'd said was supposed to make her feel better or insult her. She sighed deeply, sinking into the plastic cushion of the chair.

"I see your point," she said tersely. "But I don't have to like it, or agree with it. There are a few people, some unprejudiced, intelligent people in this town, who haven't put us in a box, taped it shut, and labeled us 'evil.'"

"I know," Fitzgibbon said with a smile. "I'm one of them."

Melody smiled back. A tremendous relief washed over her.

# Chapter
## 31

Melody pushed down the foreboding feeling she was having as she walked along the railroad tracks towards Ashby Dumping. She wished they were meeting someplace else, especially after what she'd seen there the last time. Why had he picked such a disgusting place to meet? And all along the way, it felt like something was following her. Once, she thought she heard giggling from far away.

But her excitement propelled her forward. If she didn't stay long, it was unlikely her mother and Gramps would find out she'd gone back to the restricted area to meet a boy she was forbidden to see. Besides, she hoped Van might kiss her again. The thought sent shivers through her body. That very possibility was making her do something she ordinarily wouldn't.

Van was already there. Though it was warm outside, he was wearing a long, black trench coat that made him look mysterious.

Melody quickly approached him. He took her hands in his and looked seriously into her eyes. She'd never been so eager, and so scared, in her life. He kissed her again, lightly on the lips. When he pulled back, he looked oddly confused for a moment, as if he'd forgotten why he was there.

"What's the matter?" she asked.

Van smiled. "Don't worry about me, Melody. You should never worry about me."

"But I do. In case you haven't figured it out, I *like* you."

He grinned. "I like you, too, Melody Blackstone."

"You disappeared for *days*. Where were you?"

"Home."

"You mean New York?"

Van nodded. He jumped onto the picnic table, his coat flying behind him like a cape. "Why did you go there? How did you *get* there?" Melody asked.

"The usual way," Van said, thrusting his arms out to his side, and flapping them up and down. "I *flew!*" He laughed. "There was something I needed to do."

Melody didn't like the way he avoided answering her questions directly. It made her uneasy. "I also heard you were here, in Welbourne, for some of that time. But you didn't stay with your grandfather. Where did you sleep?"

Van laughed. "Sleep doesn't matter. I can roam the night endlessly and sleep beneath the stars just because I'm thinking about you." He chuckled to himself.

Melody blushed. She knew he was acting nutty, that spending several nights sleeping outside was pretty dumb when he had a bed he could go home to. But it also sounded exciting, and Melody was intoxicated by his romance.

"How will I know if you're going to leave again?" she asked, worry in her voice.

He laughed, but Melody failed to see the humor. "I'm not going anywhere now," he promised.

She sat at the picnic table. Ashby Dumping was a filthy, dismal place. The pungent odor of something rotting was riding the wind. "What did you want to talk with me about?" she asked.

Van jumped off the table and sat next to her. He looked at her earnestly. "Did you ever feel like something was going to happen, something really important?" he asked.

Melody had those feelings all the time. So often, she couldn't count. She nodded.

"I feel like that now," he said, excitement rising in him. "I feel that an incredible power is just outside my grasp, like I can almost touch it if I reach hard enough." He took her hand again and spoke evenly. "I've started a group."

"A group? What do you mean?"

"Well, it's almost like a witches' coven. We call it a Grotto."

Melody searched Van's face for meaning, but found none. She knew what a coven was. Witches formed covens as a way of reinforcing their beliefs and helping one another. It gave them a sense of unity.

"How'd you know I was Wiccan?" she asked, seriously.

"Melody," he said, pulling her hands close to his chest. "Everyone in school knows that. I think I was here for less than a week before I found that out."

She was quiet, but her eyes were keenly focused on him.

"I needed to do this," he said. "I needed to find some explanation, some cause and effect. I want control over my life."

"Is this about your grandfather?" Melody asked suddenly.

Van didn't answer.

"It's because he's sick, isn't it?" she pressed.

He nodded, then his smile quickly drifted away.

She sighed. "He came to our house the other night. I think it was to get some advice."

For a moment a puzzled look crossed Van's face. It was quick, like a cloud passing over the sun. Then he brightened. "Isn't it ironic that our grandfathers are friends?" he asked.

Melody smiled. "It's like fate."

"Fate, that's right," Van said. "So you understand why I formed a Grotto here in Welbourne. It's fate."

She was confused. "Van," she said cautiously, taking her hand back. "I don't understand what you're talking about. What's a Grotto? Why are you telling me this?"

He leaned back and laughed. "Magic," he said finally. "I've formed a group and we practice magic. I want to take you to one of our meetings next week."

Goosebumps broke out all over Melody's body. She remembered Gramp's dark warnings about Van. "But," she hesitated, twisting her hair around her finger. "Maybe you don't understand Wiccan. I mean, people sometimes think it's only about spells and magic."

"I'm not asking you to give up anything. Just come to our meeting next Friday. It's a very important day."

Melody shook her head. It was her turn to laugh.

"Please," Van said. "What I do, and what you do, isn't so different."

"I still don't know what it is you do," she said. "You aren't Wiccan, are you?"

"No," Van said.

"Then what makes you think our beliefs are the same?"

He didn't answer.

No one had ever challenged Melody to explore a different faith, not even Bevin or Logan. She wasn't sure if she should be flattered or offended. She bit her lip, trying to imagine the benefits or consequences of what Van was asking her to do. She couldn't decide.

"I want to show you something," Van said.

He took out a small vial from his coat pocket. Inside the container was a deep green liquid. He put it in Melody's hand. She held it up to the sky, allowing the sunlight to pour through it. It was a thick and oily substance. It almost looked like perfume. She was tempted to open the top and smell it.

"What is it?" she asked.

"A very powerful potion."

Melody laughed nervously. "Well, what does it do?"

"It helps me to understand, Melody. To know the truth about everyone. Their *stories*." Then, almost to himself, he said, "When you know the stories, you have the key."

Melody gasped. The words he'd just spoken were the same ones she'd heard the little black imp say in study hall.

Giggling. Somewhere in the dump, she heard the tittering of many voices.

She stood on wobbly legs, wanting to flee.

"Let me show you," he said, thrilled. He took back the vial, still watching Melody intently. His eyes were bright, dancing with excitement. She could almost feel his body pulsating.

"I've been *chosen*," he said as he brought the vial to his lips and drank. "Perfect power awaits." His smile faltered a little as the green liquid slid down his throat and worked its way through his esophagus and into his stomach. Suddenly he began coughing.

Melody jumped up. It occurred to her that she wouldn't know what to do if the liquid were poisonous or deadly somehow. She'd seen people perform CPR on television, but she hadn't the slightest clue how to really save someone's life if she needed to.

She moved closer to Van, who was still coughing. His face was turning a deep shade of red. As she approached, his hand came up, halting her.

"Stay," he croaked.

Melody was stunned. What had he swallowed?

Van looked like he wasn't getting enough air. His hands were clutched around his neck, as though he were choking himself. His face swelled, the color turning from red to a deep purple and his eyes bulged hideously in their sockets.

Panic welled in Melody's throat. "Van!" she screamed. "What did you drink?"

Unable to speak, he waved a hand at her, motioning her to sit down again. She took another step towards him, and he backed away. He's going to die, she thought. He would die right here in Ashby Dumping and there wouldn't be anything she could do to stop it. Why had he done this? What had he wanted to prove to her?

"Van, I have to go for help!" she cried. In a sudden rush of emotion, tears sprang to her eyes and poured down her cheeks. "You can't die! I'll go get help."

She turned to leave, running full speed for the southern end of the dump, where a rusted chain-link fence guarded the entrance. Suddenly, Van was on her, throwing her to the ground hard enough to knock the wind out of her. Now it was Melody who couldn't breathe. Panicked, she sat up. Her mouth open wide, she struggled for air, clutching at her throat. Desperately, she tried sucking oxygen into her hungry lungs. Finally, she felt the relief of fresh air flowing into her body.

It took her a moment to understand what had happened, then she realized that Van, a few feet away, had stopped choking. He watched her now with the strangest expression, grinning, his eyes darting back and forth. He wasn't going to die, but now Melody feared for her own safety. Van was acting insane. Her grandfather must have been right.

In crab-like fashion, she skittered away from him. She took in thick gasps of air, unable to retreat, and fearful of what he had in mind.

In the dusty earth, he crawled towards her, his eyes wide, examining her entire body. "Look at you! It's amazing! I see right through you!" he declared, with excitement. He was looking at a skeleton. A walking skeleton, with an enormous heart.

On hands and knees, he moved to her. He touched her shoulder bone, her jaw, her knee caps. No organs. No blood, just a giant pulsating heart.

He was up close to her now, his hot breath coming in pants. Melody could see his dilated pupils. Whatever he'd swallowed, she was sure it was causing him to hallucinate.

Terrified, she only stared at him as he touched her body gingerly. "I see your heart beating," he said. It's larger than any other heart," he looked into the hollow sockets where her eyes should be. "You are truly big of heart. And it beats for me."

"Please," she said. It came out as a whisper. "Get back."

Hesitating, Van stepped back. Melody moved away, shivering violently. She stared at him. This was not the confident, sweet guy she'd met that day in The Piggy Diner. The one who'd stolen her heart. This one looked obsessed, haunted. She remembered how Logan had described him — intense. She inhaled, thankful she could breathe again. All at once, she was up on her feet, sprinting. She fled, running for her life. All the way home she felt a demon chasing her.

# Chapter
## 32

Stacey had blood on her hands. She looked around for something to wipe it off with, but could only find a small pile of moldy and decaying stuffed animals. She swiped her hands on a one-eyed teddy bear.

"Come on, Stacey!" Rudy cried with a shrill voice. "We're goin' to the cemetery to dance!" He laughed hysterically, as though this were humorous.

There was still blood on Stacey's hands and it was starting to dry. She sighed heavily, feeling frustrated and tired.

"Are you coming?" Neil asked. He had makeup on, like Rudy. Stacey barely recognized him these days. Rudy was making him into his little twin. In fact, she was beginning to think that all of them were becoming one and the same. That bothered her.

She stared at her hands.

"Did you hear me?" Neil asked, brushing against her as he followed Rudy to the railroad tracks.

"I heard you, I'll be there," she said.

She had to get the blood off somehow. She tried hard to remember what had happened earlier. Did they sacrifice a chicken, or was it a small goat? Everything was beginning to blur. The last several weeks were rolling together, one day into the next. Day turned into night, nightmares into reality. She wondered if she were losing her mind.

There was a six-pack of beer stashed inside the shed. She rushed inside, yanked a can from the pack, popped it open and let the foam fizz over. She dumped the can over her hands and scrubbed. With relief, she realized the blood was coming off.

As she left the shed, wiping her wet, sticky hands on her long black cape, she heard a voice above her.

"What a vision you are on a night like tonight," Van said.

Stacey's heart skipped, and, despite herself, she screamed.

Van jumped from the shed, his trench coat soaring above him like wings. "Did I scare you?" he asked, sarcasm tinting his question. "I'm sorry." He smiled thinly.

Stacey clutched her chest. "I was on my way to…"

"I'll walk with you," he said. He looked down at her hands. "You took the blood off. Why?"

Stacey shook her head. She watched the ground as they walked, not wanting to look into his eyes. Something strange happened when she looked into Van's eyes, like she was losing part of her soul.

Van hummed as he walked. "I like to be neat myself," he said almost to himself. "Blood is sticky and has a faint odor. It can be annoying when it gets all over you. I understand. Still, it helps us be recognized in the blackness of the night. The Lord of Darkness can track the smell to us and find us quicker."

Stacey stiffened. A small moan escaped her lips.

"What is it, Stacey? Something on your mind?"

She glared at Van. "You and Rudy… you promised us power. I thought we were going to get the things we wanted," she said, her voice strained and angry. She thought about warm and sunny Los Angeles, a place where all the beautiful people lived. No one worried about anything in L.A.

"We've done nothing lately but cut up animals. It's a bunch of sickening tricks, and the town's going crazy! They want to put us in jail forever for what we've done. If they ever find out it was us…"

"They won't," Van said confidently.

"You know, all these little sacrifices and incantations, they don't do it for me," Stacey said through clenched teeth. "If I'm risking my life, my freedom, I want more."

"I know what you want. You'll have your day in the sun," Van said and laughed. "I can promise you that when you want it enough, when the time is right, you'll go to L.A."

Stacey balked. She'd never told Van of her dream to leave Welbourne and go to Los Angeles. Maybe he found that out through Neil, although she was almost certain she'd never even told him. But one thing Van didn't know. Her time was *now*.

They walked in silence for a while. As they approached the cemetery, they could hear Rudy's high pitched wailing —his usual war-cry for fun.

Stacey stood at the gate. The wrought iron fence creaked in the wind. She could see Rudy and Neil, both dressed in black, their faces white as clowns, bobbing between tombstones. They looked like they were playing hide-and-seek. Then, Stacey saw the pentagrams — spraypainted red on several markers, like greetings at the front of the cemetery.

"Don't!" she yelled.

Van looked at her, surprised. Stacey ran after Rudy and Neil. They were giggling like children, ducking between tombstones, spraying pentagrams everywhere. She found Neil, crouching next to a stone, and knocked the can out of his hand.

"What'd you do that for?" Neil asked.

"Stop it!" Stacey commanded. "Just stop. What are you? A five year-old?"

"What's wrong with you?" Neil asked. Stacey was suddenly aware of how vacant his eyes looked. He was so lost, just following anyone who was willing to lead him around.

"What are you the cemetery police? Why should I stop?" Rudy sneered. He loomed above Stacey with a defiant look on his face, his spray-can aimed at her face.

"Because it doesn't get us anything," she lied. Their behavior was destructive and violent. She hated watching it. Everything they did lately was destructive and she was getting sick of it.

"We're in enough trouble," she said. "If we get caught doing stuff like this, stuff we don't even *need* to do... well, I'm not going down for you two idiots."

"She's right," Van said.

Rudy looked perplexed. "Excuse me. Wasn't it you that started this pentagram-writing on tombstones?"

"That was different," Van said. "There was a good reason for it then."

"Which was?" Rudy said.

"Nothing for you to know about now," Van said, snipping the conversation. He dumped the black gym bag he'd been carrying onto the ground. "Is there anyone else who wants to add to our collection?" he asked, pointing to the bag. "Come on, we only have a week until the holiday, and I still have to put everything together for our ceremony."

Stacey took a small paper bag out of the pocket of her cape and unceremoniously dumped it into the gym bag. Neil was next. Reaching into the pockets of his denim jacket, he pulled out a plastic container with something that sloshed as he handed it to Van.

"Is that everything off the sheet of paper I gave all of you?" Van asked, a smirk developing at the side of his mouth.

"That's everything on my list," Stacey said, her eyes small and tight.

"Me, too," Neil said.

Van looked at Rudy. "I told you, man. I was done yesterday. Ain't nothing left on my list."

Van bent and zippered the bag shut.

"Aren't you gonna tell us what this spell or ritual is?" Rudy asked eagerly.

Van couldn't help but smile, his mouth displaying every one of his teeth. "It's a wonderful surprise for all of you," he said happily. "Believe me, you won't be disappointed."

Stacey folded her hands in front of her. "I have a question, too," she said looking at Van. "When are you going to initiate our new member?"

Van's smile faltered slightly. "I told you, she's not going to be a member," he said. "You'll see her on Walpurgisnacht. Everything is under control."

Stacey doubted it. She looked from face to face. They were members of a Grotto. She was one of them. She should have felt close to them, connected by a pledge and their recent misdeeds. But instead, she was feeling more and more isolated. She felt as if she were stranded on a deserted island with her worst enemies.

Van watched Stacey, knowing her commitment was faltering. What was he going to do about her? Suddenly he heard giggling at his feet. Cold, bare flesh brushed against him. He looked down and saw a plump black creature dart behind a tombstone. Van's heart leapt.

"Did you see it?" he asked Stacey.

She turned to him, puzzled. "See what?"

"One of... Satan's minions." He laughed, clapping his hands together. "They've come. I can *see* them now. Do you know what this means?" he asked, turning towards her.

Baffled, Stacey only stared back.

"It means the power is mine."

From somewhere in the cemetery, he heard the intimate, familiar voice, "The Devil is looking for you," it said.

Van chuckled. "I know. And I'm looking for him," he replied.

# Chapter
## 33

Wearing their Sunday best, the three women stood for a moment in the doorway of the diner, Bibles gripped tightly in their hands. It was lunchtime, when The Piggy Diner was its busiest. Slowly, patrons took notice of the silent women who stood watching the crowd from the doorway. The steady hum of conversations quieted, along with the clinking of glasses and silverware on plates. One of the three, an elderly woman wearing a black hat, looked at each patron, as if calculating their particular measure of virtue.

Leotie was pouring another cup of coffee for Joshua Briggs. The sudden drop in the diner's noise level made her look up, locking eyes with the old woman. She stretched one arm out with the Bible in her hand, then placed the other hand on top of the Good Book, swinging it slowly around, waiting for all the patrons to look at her.

"Do we not all want to dwell in the house of the Lord?" she asked. People watched the women with dull expressions, some still chewing their food, others whispering into their lunch-mates' ears.

"Is this not what we all want? To be with our Lord Jesus Christ when we die? To live in His Kingdom, in Heaven, with our families and loved ones forever?"

Someone at the back of the diner yelled out, "I do."

Leotie looked back at the kitchen. Frannie Landers was coming out, wiping her hands on a dish towel, her forehead wrinkled with concern.

"What's going on?" Leotie whispered to Frannie.

Frannie shrugged. "They're CWO," she whispered back. Leotie wondered what three women from the Christian Women's Organization were doing at The Piggy Diner.

The old woman with the Bible looked like she should be having tea with her friends instead of preaching the gospel to a bustling diner. But she knew how to work the crowd. She paced the floor, looking from face to face. "Lord, sinners though we may be, we call on You for help. We need You today more than we ever have before, and dear Lord, You know why. There are people here in our town doing great evil." She looked searchingly. "We all know it, do we not?"

Several people nodded, frowning.

"It's here in the Bible, friends! Ezekiel, chapter 33, verses 6 to 9." The old woman cracked the binding of her Bible and read, "'When I say unto the wicked, O wicked man, thou shalt surely die; if thou dost not speak to warn the wicked from his way, that wicked man shall die in his iniquity.'"

She stopped. The room was now completely quiet. The old woman turned and looked steadily at Leotie.

Leotie swallowed hard. It was clear why the women had come to The Piggy Diner. They were there to see Leotie, to make accusations and to expose her as a heathen. All eyes in the crowded diner had turned to her. She briskly wiped her hands on her apron and shifted nervously. But she held the old woman's gaze, not looking away. She didn't want to appear intimidated, although that's exactly how she felt.

Warm hands on hers, comforting. She looked down at Joshua Briggs. He sat, quiet and unfazed at the counter, a half-eaten piece of apple pie and a cup of hot coffee in front of him. He smiled at Leotie.

"Pay them no mind," he said firmly. He blew on his coffee mug and ventured a sip. His back faced the CWO women, and he did not turn around to give them the benefit of his attention. His eyes were steady on Leotie.

She smiled back, drawing strength from her friend. Joshua, always practical and sensible. He was a smart, kind-hearted soul who didn't rattle easily.

Leotie felt the tension begin to loosen in her back as she worked to consciously make the negative feelings melt away. She turned to the sink, intent on getting back to her job.

"Idolatry!" The word rang out, deafening in the silence. It made Leotie jump in spite of herself. The old woman let the word hang in the air. "Witchcraft, my friends, is *forbidden* by God!" she cried, her voice thick with accusation. "There are witches who live among us! If our livestock and pets are not safe, are our children and our grandchildren safe? Are any of us safe when these detestable practices are happening here in our community?"

Leotie was drying dishes. Her hands shook as she wrapped a dishcloth around a wet coffee mug. The old woman's words besieged her. She looked intently at the cup she was drying, feeling the anger in the air, and the gentle eyes of Joshua Briggs upon her.

"It's here in the Bible! 'Let no one be found among you who practices divination or sorcery, interprets omens, engages in witchcraft or casts spells...'" Leotie dropped the coffee mug. It crashed loudly to the floor, shattering into pieces. "...'or who is a medium or spiritualist or who consults the dead. Anyone who does these things is detestable to the Lord, and because of these detestable practices, the Lord your God will drive out those nations before you. You must be blameless before the Lord your God.'"

Leotie looked up to confront the old woman, whose lips were pursed tightly together. She stared directly at her, her heart beating furiously with anger. The woman took two steps closer to Leotie. Now they were only a few feet away from each other.

"*Your* Lord, *your* God — not mine," Leotie said. She bit each word off, letting them cut the air like a knife. "My god is not an angry god. My goddess is not a punitive goddess. I answer only to my own moral conscience and convictions."

"Witch!" someone hissed.

Leotie leaned into the counter and looked around the diner. These were her neighbors, her customers, her friends. She had nothing to hide, not from them, and never from herself.

"That's right. I'm a witch! My family and I are practicing Wiccans. But do you know what that means? Do you?" She looked from face to face. They all looked away.

"Means you're a sorceress or something!" someone shouted.

Leotie looked around, locating the voice. It was someone she didn't know. A large man with a burly beard, wearing a red checkered shirt.

"No. You're wrong. It's sad that you use words to describe people but you have no idea what the terms really mean, or what the people you're labeling are really like. It makes me angry and it makes me sad.

"Wiccans live and let live. We practice rituals and spells to align ourselves with nature. We acknowledge a depth of power far greater than that apparent to the average person, and *that* we consider being magic. It's only the natural potential in us all."

Leotie looked to a woman sitting with her daughters at a table near the counter. "We would *never* slaughter your animals. And, if we love our own children so deeply, more than we even love ourselves, how could we ever harm someone else's?"

The old woman's eyes darted across the quiet room, looking for alliance.

"We're not bound by your traditions, by your allegiance to the almighty God from your Bible. But that doesn't make us evil. On the contrary, we're loving, good people. We honor the earth and the powers of the universe."

The mother at the table smiled brightly at Leotie. "I think that sounds lovely," she said.

"It is," Briggs replied, finally turning around from the counter. He smiled back at the woman and her children.

Frannie Landers finally had to speak up. This had gone on long enough. She was tired of all the fussing in her diner. "Thank y'all for stopping in," she said, hands on her large hips. "We much appreciate the Bible study, but folks need to be focusing on eatin' my delicious crabapple pie right now."

The three women shifted uncomfortably. The old woman hesitated, then nodded reluctantly to her two cohorts. They began walking to the door. "Be sure to let us know when the next CWO bake sale is now," Frannie said as she ushered them politely but firmly to the door. "We'll be proud to send you over a dozen pies."

The old woman was the last to leave. Her companions were on the sidewalk, waiting, but she paused in the doorway, raised a gloved hand and turned to eye Leotie a final time. "You will not inherit the Kingdom of the Lord," she said flatly.

"No," Leotie said. "I will inherit a much kinder kingdom."

# Chapter
## 34

Welbourne was up in arms over the desecration of the cemetery and the animal mutilation crimes. In every way possible, the citizens of the town were putting the heat on the Sheriff's office to find and arrest the perpetrators.

Sheriff Larkin and Principal Fitzgibbon seemed to be the only ones who suspected Van Masterson. Fitzgibbon's suspicions were aroused when he noticed Masterson hanging around with Rudy Nobel, Neil Carey, and Stacey Malone, three teenagers with troubled histories and bad reputations.

As for the Sheriff, he had a hunch, based on nothing but instinct, that Masterson was involved in this sad crime wave. His instincts, however, came from years of experience in law enforcement, and he trusted them fully. And if he was right, he was sure the boy was capable of worse crimes than cutting up chickens.

The Sheriff and Deputy Sheriff asked Van to come in for questioning. The boy brought his grandfather along, but no lawyer. They didn't read him his rights; so far, they didn't know enough to arrest anybody.

Larkin hoped the boy would be nervous and let something slip. But Van was cool and composed. He listened courteously to each question and thought carefully before answering. There was none of the restlessness, fear, or anger that innocent people usually showed when they were being questioned. The kid was too much in control for it to be natural.

While young Van was putting on his act, Larkin kept his eyes on Mr. Masterson's face. The elderly man sat quietly next to his grandson, his hands clasped tightly in front of him. He was there as the boy's advocate, but he looked unconvincing in his role. All in all, the Sheriff was sure the boy was hiding something. Larkin decided to go looking for what that was.

Leaving the Sheriff's office, Van walked as quickly as he could. He hated cops, even when they were called "Sheriff," and he couldn't get away from the county jail fast enough. His grandfather, arthritic and fatigued, struggled to catch up with him.

"Hold on," the senior croaked behind him. "Hold on there, got somethin' to tell ya."

Van came to a halt. He looked back at his grandfather with disdain. "Well?" he said, impatiently.

Huffing laboriously, Masterson shuffled up to his grandson. He looked into his cold eyes and swallowed hard.

"Hurry up, old man," Van complained. "I've got things to do."

"I got somethin' important to tell ya," the senior Masterson said. "I have to tell ya 'cause maybe it'll help ya. I messed up real good with my own son. And I didn't do so great even with my own life. But, Van, I done things when I was your age. Things kinda like you're doin'."

"How - do - you - know - what - I'm - doing?" Van said, biting off each word, his hateful eyes narrowing.

"I know! I may be old, but I ain't stupid! You're up to no good. I did things, too, is what I'm tryin' to tell ya! I did things almost like what you're doin' now. And I ended up regrettin' it," he said.

"What are you telling me?" Van asked, his curiosity piqued. "That you did magic?"

"Somethin' like that. It was just once. Just one spell. We did it at Ashby Dumpin'. That filthy, wicked place just attracts evil! See, I really loved this girl," he tried to explain. "It was called a revealing spell, that's what Earl done told me. Got me to do it with 'im... to see which one she truly cared fer.

"I thought it was gonna be Earl Blackstone. Course," he said with a laugh, "Earl thought it was gonna be me! But as it turned out, it weren't neither of us. She loved someone else. And all the spell revealed was that she liked him too.

"But this other man... he weren't worthy of her love. This other man weren't worthy of taking out her trash. He saw that she was interested in him and he went after her, trying to force himself on her. He almost hurt her real bad. Me and Earl, we came upon them, lucky thing. Though Earl said that was part of the spell. We *helped* her."

Trying to catch his breath, he stopped to unbutton the top button of his shirt. He was breathing heavily. His grandson watched with removed interest.

"Then the law came... and then came goin' to court," he said, breathlessly, continuing his story. "Earl and I found ourselves witnesses to that wickedness. And *she...* she suddenly denied it all! Jes like that!"

"The next thing we knew, she up and married him! Made me and Earl look like liars. After that, I did like the Good Book tells us. No more messin' with witchcraft. I stuck to the church, and kept outta people's business. Let 'em take care of their own, I'd say." He paused, a deep sigh expelling from his dry lips. "I thought I knew everythin'. Thought I was smart.

"Earl was different though. Nothin' ever seemed to rattle that old geezer." He smiled. "Still the same today. Still cares for everyone. Close to his faith. Close to his family."

"So you cast a spell," Van said, incredulously. He stared at his grandfather, arms across his chest. "My grandfather! The Baptist man of God! And it blew up in your face!" he laughed out loud. "Well, now! Isn't that just divine intervention?"

"Van," the old man warned. "Heed my advice, boy. Don't think ya know so much—when ya do, God will surely humble you. And ya won't like the way He'll do it, neither!"

# Chapter
## 35

Sipping black coffee, Leotie stared at Melody from the kitchen window. She wanted to get up and put sugar in her cup, but was reluctant to pull herself away from this silent brooding. Outside, Melody sat listlessly on the lawn, watching Annabelle cluck at her feet and occasionally tossing the chicken a handful of cracked corn. She'd been sullen and quiet for over a week, even claiming she had a cold so she'd have an excuse to stay home from school.

The only one Melody had talked to recently was Bevin, who'd called the house phone on Thursday. Leotie asked Bevin why she hadn't called Melody's cell phone, and Bevin told her all her calls had gone to voice mail, so she assumed Melody had turned her cell off.

This gave Leotie a chance to overhear part of the girls' conversation. Apparently a girl named Maureen had been diagnosed with migraines so severe that she was taking a leave of absence for the rest of the semester. For some reason, this information bothered Melody, who became even quieter and more morose, shutting herself up in her bedroom for long hours.

Leotie asked her about it. Melody would only say that in some way, she felt responsible.

Leotie was worried. Her daughter had never acted like this before. It was Friday, and Leotie told Frannie she was taking the weekend off. She hoped that spending some time with Melody might help her find out what was bothering her daughter.

Things had been hard since her husband's death. But she was proud of the way they'd all kept it together, and thankful that her family found productive ways of coping with the pain of their loss.

But they still mourned. Melody's moodiness, and the sometimes ear-splitting silence between the two of them was evident of that. Still, it was unusual for Melody to be this withdrawn.

The previous Wednesday, Leotie had come home from work to find Melody locked in her bedroom. She wouldn't come out, and refused to go to school. She slept the days away, barely eating, barely speaking. Leotie could see she was depressed, but her daughter pushed her away, refusing to share whatever problems were troubling her.

Remembering that afternoon, Leotie felt certain that something had happened that day to Melody.

"Something ain't right," Earl said suddenly from behind her, speaking her thoughts as if they were words written across the window.

Leotie gave a start. "Oh! I guess I was so deep in thought I didn't even hear you come into the kitchen." She shook her head. "You're right. Something's wrong." She took another sip of coffee. "I just don't know what it is, or how to fix it."

"Maybe Melody's just going through one of them stages," Earl offered dubiously, though Leotie knew he didn't hold with ideas like that.

"I suppose that could be it," she answered with a sigh. She gave Earl a look from over the rim of her cup. She could always tell when he was holding back. "You might as well say it," she nudged. "You know you'll end up speaking your mind sooner or later. What do you think is going on?"

"Might be Van Masterson's grandson is what's making her so confused and unhappy," Earl said. "She seems mighty taken with him. She won't listen to a word I've said about being careful of that boy." He poured himself a cup of coffee from the pot on the stove.

A hundred worst-case scenarios went through Leotie's mind. "You don't think he's gotten her involved in Satanism, do you?" she demanded, as if Earl had the answers.

"Don't think we should be thinking thoughts like that, now," Earl said, a bit alarmed. He put an arm around his daughter-in-law and hugged her tightly. "She's a good girl. And she's smart, too. You know your daughter. She's not one to make reckless decisions."

Leotie looked back out the window just in time to see Melody making her way towards the wheat field, probably on her way to the altar.

"I hope you're right," Leotie said. She took a deep breath and exhaled. "You know, we're coming upon the anniversary of his death."

Earl nodded. As if he needed any reminding.

"Maybe that's what's making her act like this," she said.

"Could be," Earl said quietly.

"Anyway, I can't drive myself crazy with frightful possibilities. I have to *know* what's really bothering her."

Earl turned away and began rummaging in the cupboards, looking for something sweet to eat with his coffee. "Then you're going to have to talk with her," he said.

"I've tried. She won't tell me."

"Try a different approach. That's what faith is for."

Leotie looked up at him and smiled. Earl was right. She couldn't remember the last time she'd spent time with Melody practicing their sacred Wiccan rites. Being so busy, she'd neglected many of their holidays. Even today. It was Beltane, a holiday that celebrated the merging of the Goddess and the God, and the passing of the Young God into manhood. It was a time for May Poles and a favorite time for handfasting and Wiccan marriage ceremonies. It was a special holiday and she hadn't even acknowledged it to her daughter. She felt a pang of guilt.

Leotie remembered when Melody was a little girl. They used to spend hours together singing ancient songs, making home-brewed herbal teas and performing rituals to attune themselves with the natural rhythm of life forces. Those days seemed long ago. Now she was a single parent, and as the sole financial provider for their household, she worked long hours. After work, she paid bills, caught up on laundry, housekeeping, and the general daily chores of life. She had to let some things go.

Melody was more important. Her faith was more important. She promised herself that when her daughter came back, they'd celebrate the holiday together, as it was meant to be celebrated.

Leotie looked back out the window. Melody was gone, some strands of wheat lightly trampled at the spot where she'd entered the field.

# Chapter
## 36

Melody was already halfway to the altar. For over a week, she'd wanted nothing more than to be alone, to meditate and try to find answers to way too many questions. Her life felt like it was spiraling out of control. Either that, or her visions, the constant accusations and ridicule at school, and, of course, the suspicious way her father had died, were taking its toll and making her crazy.

Lately, she'd pushed the boundaries of her otherwise routine life. She'd performed forbidden spells, witnessed secret animal sacrifices, talked to a dead man in her dream, and seen frightening visions outside of her meditations and trances.

Somehow, she must have become clairvoyant, developing some type of extrasensory perception. Otherwise, she wouldn't have been able to have seen the interloper in the cemetery digging up the grave, the predator chasing the cat that — she knew now — must have been prey. Giggling black imps and divinatory statements — she had no idea what it all meant, or why it was happening to *her*.

Her grandfather had told her that Van Masterson was involved in something bad. She sighed wearily. The image of Van drinking that green liquid, his crazy, hostile actions. Melody shivered. How could he have said the very words that were spoken to her in a vision?

Then she thought of his deep blue eyes, the way he touched her. The way he made her feel. She wanted to be with him, but –

A terrible thought occurred to her. What if the love spell she'd done had come back three times? What if, knowing she was a witch, and wanting to impress her, Van had consumed that poisonous drink, thinking it'd provide him with some type of magical powers?

She felt a shiver of guilt. Maybe her spell had somehow robbed him of his free will. What if he was acting crazy out of love? If her spell had worked, maybe she was responsible for Van's emotional instability. This was the kind of consequence her grandfather tried to warn her about.

If only to assure herself that Van was just a normal guy, and that what had happened at Ashby Dumping was just a fluke, she wanted to see him again. But not now. Now she wanted time to sort things out.

She saw the altar. It stood solemn, a beacon to her soul. Just looking at it filled her with a soothing peace. She sat on the ground with her back to the stone, closed her eyes, focused her breathing and began meditating. She hadn't realized how exhausted she was. When her body finally relaxed, the culmination of several sleepless nights and anxiety caught up with her. She slumped to the earth, fast asleep.

---

Melody woke with a start. She must have been asleep a couple of hours because the sky was already darkening. She stretched, yawned and stood up. For the first time in days, she felt restored.

Then she heard a familiar voice. Unguarded and still groggy from sleep, she thought her heart literally skipped a beat.

"You look so peaceful when you sleep," Van Masterson said.

She turned around. A little scream escaped her mouth. Van stood at the edge of the field behind the altar. He was wearing his long black trench coat and holding a large bouquet of wildflowers. He was smiling, but his eyes looked troubled. "I'm sorry! I didn't mean to scare you," he said, moving closer. "That's why I waited for you to wake up!"

"You were watching me sleep?" Melody asked, alarmed. She scanned the wheat field, her eyes roaming over the clearing of cottonwood trees. There was no one else around. "How did you find me here?"

"I followed you," he said. Walking towards her, he handed her the bouquet. Melody took the flowers without looking at them; her gaze fixed on his face.

"You followed me?" she stammered.

"I was worried about you."

Melody stood rigidly clutching the flowers. "Why?"

"You haven't been in school in over a week. No one could reach you. Wouldn't you worry if that were me?"

"Like when you disappeared without anyone knowing where *you* were?"

"I see your point."

"If I were sick or in trouble, don't you think my family would do something about it? Why are you *really* here?"

He took Melody's hand and looked at it, as though it were a rare and precious object. Slowly he turned it over and pressed his warm lips to her palm. "I needed to see you," he breathed. "I missed you. I thought we felt the same about each other."

Looking into his crystal blue eyes, the original attraction reasserted itself. Melody felt a warm, pulsating sensation through her entire body. Flustered, she didn't know whether to welcome him... or elude him.

As much as she wanted him to hold her, she also wanted to be alone, to try and sort things out. Maybe Van had nothing to do with what was happening to her lately, but seeing him confused her.

She pulled her hand away and tried to swallow the lump growing in her throat. "Van," she said cautiously. "At Ashby Dumping the other day..." He watched her quietly, waiting for her to continue. "What you did, that stuff you swallowed... you acted kind of crazy. The things you said didn't make any sense."

"Haven't people ever looked at you like you were crazy?" he asked. "When you pray to your Goddess, or dance under a full moon, don't people think you're nuts?"

Melody hesitated. He had a point. "But what did you drink?"

"Don't you believe in magic?"

"Of course, but..."

"You know the Native Americans sometimes smoke peyote in their religious ceremonies. It happens to be a hallucinogen derived from cactus. Do you think that's crazy?"

"Well, I dunno, no, I guess..." Melody said, thinking of her own Kiowa ancestry.

"Many different religions embrace altered states of mind. What do you think prayer is all about?"

Melody considered a moment. He seemed so sensible, rational. He took her hands and held them in his own.

"I'm sorry if I scared you the other day," he said, wondering if she could see the deceit in his eyes. When she embraced him, he knew she hadn't.

"You scared me," she whispered, clinging to him. "But there's way more going on in my life that's been scaring me, too. I don't know how to handle things anymore. The town thinks I've been doing those animal sacrifices. I had nothing to do with them!"

"I know."

"I wanted to tell someone at the beginning, but I was afraid," Melody continued. "The kids at school won't let up. They harass me every day of my life! And it's just been getting worse. Even my mom is being tormented. She had a dead chicken thrown at her,

her tires slashed, and some crazy CWO woman shouting at her at work. On top of that..." Melody stopped, her gaze drifting away then coming back to Van. "It's the anniversary of my dad's death."

Van pulled Melody to him, and she yielded to the comfort of his arms. He looked earnestly into her eyes and then kissed her. She let herself be taken by the moment, her body melting.

"I'm sorry about your dad. I want to help in some way," he said.

"I came out here to the altar because it's Beltane. It's a holiday for us, and no one at home even said a word about it."

"Then we should celebrate Beltane together."

Suddenly she remembered a conversation she'd had with Van about some type of group he was forming, a Grotto, and how he'd wanted her to come to a meeting. Was that tonight?

"You'd celebrate a Wiccan holiday?" Melody asked, skeptically.

"Yeah. It sounds cool."

"Won't that mess with whatever religion you practice... like... well, what religion are you?" She hadn't asked the question very eloquently, but she needed to know the answer.

"I'm agnostic." Van lied. "I've never been baptized. Is that all right with you?"

She smiled. "Sure. That's fine with me."

"So, what do we do?" he asked.

"Well, Beltane is a kind of a fertility holiday," she explained. She put a hand up to her mouth and blushed.

Van smirked. "Sounds fascinating. What do I have to do?"

Melody laughed. "When I was a little girl, we used to put up a Maypole and sing and dance around it. But that was a long time ago. We don't do that anymore. Mostly, we just present flowers to the altar, pray. Sometimes we'll do spells for a bountiful crop. Beltane's also a time for Wiccan marriages." She blushed again. "I mean, if there were two witches who wanted to get married, Beltane's a good day to do that." Her face grew hotter.

"I have an idea," Van said, a smile spreading across his face.

"Yeah?"

"Well, you have to come with me."

Melody looked up at the darkening sky and frowned. "I'm not sure I can. I've been gone for awhile and my mom and Gramps will probably be worried about me."

"This won't take long, I promise!"

She shook her head. "I don't know."

"Come on, Melody," Van encouraged. "Don't you want to do some of the things you did when you were little?" He kissed her cheek. "Humor me a little."

"We'll come right back here?"

"I promise," Van said, and then he crossed his heart.

# Chapter
## ❧37❧

It didn't take Larkin long to find out about Van Masterson's troubled past. His name came up quickly on the Sheriff's central database, listing all his prior arrests — breaking and entering, assault, and petty larceny.

Early in his career, Masterson had been ordered to perform 300 hours of community service in the Bronx, where he lived with his father. The record showed he hadn't met his commitment. No surprise. A year later, he'd spent time in a juvenile detention home. There was also some disturbing information about his psychological profile. Apparently, the boy had been institutionalized a few times—the terms "bipolar" and "schizophrenia" were scattered throughout his file.

From what he'd read, it appeared that Van Masterson was an intelligent, articulate, seemingly well-mannered teenager with psychological problems and a juvenile record.

Principal Fitzgibbon told the Sheriff that the boy's IQ was extremely high. The Sheriff couldn't help but think what a shame it was that Van had gotten himself involved in deviant activities. Perhaps if his childhood had been different, things might have worked out better for him. But Larkin often thought that when he encountered troubled teens. And the truth was that wasn't always the case. In his career, he'd seen some of the best kids come out of terrible homes. And, some kids, who had every opportunity in the world, tossed it all away on drugs and crime. The Sheriff had come to believe that, at a certain point, people created their own fate.

Finding out that Welbourne's newest resident was a convicted criminal wasn't what disturbed Sheriff Larkin the most — it was talking to the boy's father.

The father had been a little hard to track down. The Sheriff started by calling the home number listed in the police reports. No one ever seemed to be home, and there was no answering machine, no listed cell phones. The only other phone number in Van's records, this one from his school files, was for a neighbor named Pete Wilcox.

Wilcox was easy enough to reach. He not only gave the Sheriff the name of a local bar, suggesting that the father might be there, but a brief history of Van's upbringing. Apparently Van's parents separated when he was only seven years old, and his mother died shortly after that, a car accident. Van had lived with his father ever since.

Following Wilcox's tip, the Sheriff located Van's father, Walter Masterson, at the joint where he tended bar.

Larkin was polite and curt, "I'm sorry to bother you at work, Mr. Masterson. I'm Sheriff Larkin from the Cowley County Sheriff's Office in Welbourne."

Masterson wasn't surprised by the call. "What'd my son do now?" he asked with a grunt.

"If I could just take a moment to explain the situation..."

Walt Masterson interrupted him. "I sent him all the way to that hick town just to keep him out of trouble," he complained. The Sheriff could hear him puffing on a cigarette. He blew smoke into the phone. "I mean, Welbourne, for God's sake! What trouble could he get into in Welbourne?"

The Sheriff was momentarily silent. He'd been under the impression that Van Masterson had been sent to Welbourne to care for his grandfather, a recluse who was aging and quickly deteriorating in health. At least that was the story Van had fed his classmates, a story that had quickly gotten back to Fitzgibbon and then to Larkin.

"I'm sorry, Mr. Masterson. I think there's a misunderstanding..."

"Yeah well..." More smoke blew into the receiver. "There's no misunderstanding that my kid's a thief. So, what'd he steal now? Don't tell me some poor farmer's cows or something!" He snorted. "That'd just be a kick in the pants. Hey, he's not in some cult again, is he?"

"Had Van been involved in a cult in New York?"

"He didn't tell you that? I'm surprised his grandfather didn't say nothin'. He's so damn proud of how I raised my son, you know," Walter said sarcastically. Suddenly the Sheriff heard a blast of loud music through the telephone.

"Hang on a second..." He cuffed the phone. The Sheriff could hear him yelling at someone at the bar. There was muffled conversation and then the music stopped. "Sorry 'bout that. Where was I? Oh, yeah, the cult he was in. Real weird stuff, you know. I don't know how the hell he got himself into that stuff. He's a smart kid. A little crazy, though... kinda talks to people who aren't there. Did you know he's a genius? Yeah, well, it probably didn't come up in conversation.

"Anyhow, they were into devil worship, stuff like that, him and these kids he hung around with. I thought it was nothing, myself. I mean, sometimes kids do that stuff, you know. I did some stupid things when I was Van's age." Walter chuckled. His laugh turned into a hacking cough. He took a long draw from his cigarette and continued. "Well, anyway, it turned out to be some heavy stuff they were gettin' into.

"They were taking strays off the street, and, you know, sacrificing them. They all dressed in black. It was beginning to look like Halloween every night around my apartment when all his friends came over.

"Then I thought about Welbourne. God, I hated that town. No offense, Sheriff, but I couldn't wait to get the hell out of there, get away from my dad. I thought, maybe if I sent him to my dad — he had a way making you do what you're supposed to. With me, it was his belt. You know, whack! Anyway, I figured maybe he'd stay out of trouble at least until he could graduate from high school. Then, he's an adult and can do whatever he pleases, it ain't my responsibility.

"I mean *Kansas*. How much trouble could he get into there?" He laughed again. The Sheriff heard him swallow from a drink. "So," Walter continued. "What did the kid do, anyhow?"

Sheriff Larkin paused a moment. "We're not sure yet, Mr. Masterson. There were some animal mutilations in town. We think he may be a part of it."

"Are you gonna arrest him?"

"Not yet. We brought him in for questioning. He's denied any involvement."

The sound of glass breaking. The noise in the bar began to rise. "Sorry, Sheriff, I gotta go," Walter said. "Can you do me a favor, though?"

"If I can."

"Maybe you better check up on my old man. I'm not sure how seriously he takes Van."

# Chapter
## 38

Sheriff Larkin was still mulling over the short sad history of Van as he headed out to the Masterson home. He didn't bother calling first. Everyone knew the elderly man didn't have a phone and that he rarely left his property.

It was just getting dark outside when he pulled into the gravel driveway. Several tumbleweeds rolled next to his car. He got out of his cruiser and hollered his arrival. In these parts, creeping up unannounced on a person's property could get you shot. "Hello there, Van," he called. "It's Sheriff Larkin."

Old man Masterson lived in a ramshackle little house. He had several acres of land that had once grown alfalfa and corn, but it was overgrown now with weeds and prairie grass.

The screen door creaked as the Sheriff opened it. He knocked on the inner door and waited. Give the man time, he thought. Getting older, like he was, it might be hard for him to get to the door. After a while passed and there was no sound of anyone home, he knocked again, this time harder. No one came to the door.

"Van?" he hollered, louder now. "It's the Sheriff. Could you open the door?"

No one answered.

"Mr. Masterson, I'm going to open the door now, sir. I need to make sure you're all right." The Sheriff tried the door, not surprised to find it unlocked. Most Welbourne residents kept their doors unlocked all hours of the day and night.

The door opened up into a small kitchen. A trash bag sat open on the floor by the sink, food decaying inside.

"Mr. Masterson, I'm in the house now," the Sheriff said, mostly to himself. He was relatively certain no one was home. An eerie feeling swept over him at the thought of maybe finding the old man lying dead on the couch or in his bed.

Two kitchen chairs were lying on the floor, looking like they'd been knocked down. Instantly, he was put on alarm. A struggle? He pulled out his weapon, and with extra caution, crept to the den. The TV was on, but the sound was down.

An old recliner faced the television. On a TV tray next to the chair was a full plate of macaroni and cheese, congealed and cold. The Sheriff quickly made his way to the room on the right, a small bedroom with a double bed. The room was stuffy and smelled stale. He checked under the bed and in the closet. No one.

He left the bedroom, went back through the den, and entered another even smaller bedroom that might once have been a storage room. In the corner, boxes were piled high to the ceiling. A dresser and an unmade twin bed, covers tumbled in a heap, were the only clues that someone was occupying the room. The Sheriff checked the tiny closet and under the bed. Satisfied that there was no one in the house, he was about to leave when something caught his eye.

Under a pile of clothes, he saw the corner of a black object. He bent down to retrieve it and found a small hardwood box. A small clasp held it closed, but it wasn't locked. Inside was a leather-bound journal.

Sheriff Larkin opened the pages to the junior Van Masterson's diary and was immediately drawn into a private world of black magic. On the creamy bond paper, Van gave an intimate portrait of his life. His words were articulate and passionate as he described, sometimes in morbid detail, the progression of his involvement in Satanism.

The journal was started several years ago, when Van joined a club that purported to teach teenagers about transcendental meditation. Van joined because he hungered for friendships and yearned for things that would challenge him. At school, he was a shy, quiet loner. His classes bored him. His teachers admired his intelligence, but lamented the fact that he didn't even try to work up to his potential. The students avoided him, detesting his shyness, or envying his abilities. Even his father didn't think he was important enough to spend time with.

At TMC — the Transcendental Meditation Club — Van finally began to feel a connection. He met other teens his own age from all different walks of life. The classes were enjoyable, and the members were friendly, eager to include him in their activities. He'd found a social comfort zone, gained friends, and soon was the happiest he'd been in his entire life. What he didn't realize was that the group, set up as an educational forum, was really a cult.

After the TMC gained the confidence of its new members, the brainwashing began. They used techniques like thought-stopping, a process to control the thoughts of followers through meditation, and speaking in tongues. They also used a staring technique, where members would gaze into each other's eyes without blinking for a prolonged period of time, putting them into a deep trance and making them susceptible to suggestion.

The cult preyed on people who were smart, creative and non-conformists, but, generally speaking, misfits. Members were emotionally manipulated into believing that the TMC was a clan that accepted and appreciated them. It was their only real family.

TMC was in the business of making money. The purpose of their mind-control was to create an army of teenage criminals. All the spoils benefited the cult. Van and the other TMC members robbed gas stations, electronic stores and laundry mats

— any place they could quickly make off with cash or high-end commodities that could be sold easily on the street.

Then Van got caught. TMC members never talked about the cult. They took the blame, and after they got out of jail, or detention center, they went right back to TMC.

On a certain level, Van was aware of TMC's schemes. But he was in deep. It was the first time in his life that he ever felt he belonged. His mother had abandoned him when he was only seven, leaving him with an alcoholic, abusive father. And she died before Van had any type of closure with her. Her desertion and untimely death left a chasm in Van's heart and soul, causing irrevocable damage. He never felt that he was loved or important.

He wanted out of the cult, but at the same time, he didn't think he could do it. He was like a junkie. He needed the feeling of belonging that he got from the group, the sense of purpose to what otherwise felt like a life adrift.

At TMC he met three other boys a few years older than himself, and they offered a way out. With their help, Van broke away from TMC, only to join them in another cult—a Satanic one. They drew Van into the new group as easily as a moth to a light. They offered him power, immense knowledge, and popularity — the very things Van craved. They asked for nothing from him — not at first.

Slowly things got serious. The Grotto grew to fifteen members and started collecting stray cats off the streets of New York. In an abandoned, dilapidated building — rats scurrying beneath their feet and the subway storming by — they sacrificed the animals to their newfound god. They chanted. They drank blood. They read from the *Black Book of Satan* and performed ritualistic magic.

Then the abductions started. At first, Van wanted nothing to do with them. He threatened to leave the Grotto, but he was more a part of things than he wanted to admit, and he stayed.

In a beat-up Chevy van, he watched through a dirty window when members kidnapped a fifteen-year-old girl on her way home from school. He said nothing when they left her, bound and blindfolded, in an abandoned apartment without food or water. He laughed when they taunted her, poked her with sticks, and forced her to eat bugs. And nights later, when they released her, hysterical and dazed in a secluded part of Central Park, he did nothing to help her find her way home.

There were several kidnappings after that, always the same. Nameless, frightened girls who were tormented and ridiculed and forced to participate in rituals — drinking animal blood, watching the teens make sacrifices to the dark lord — and then released days later in a state of shock and panic.

Like a dream, Van sometimes watched and sometimes participated in the Grotto's activities. He often felt like he was someone else — a character in a movie. He watched himself from the outside, feeling what the others' felt — the excitement and adventure — but always from a safe distance. It was fantasy. His mind drifted outside his body and he believed that, like a movie, he could always rewind his actions and start from the beginning again if he wanted. Without a conscience, he could participate without repercussions.

Soon, Fabian Osgood, the high priest, began bringing a woman in her early twenties to their meetings. Mia Chung was her name. Osgood said she was an important addition to their Grotto. He told them she had magnificent powers, passed down to her through her family of Chinese descent. She knew ancient and mighty secrets that she imparted to Osgood.

About the same time that Mia came on board, Van's father caught wind of his son's involvement in the Satanic cult. He searched Van's room and found books on Satanism and demonic possession, black candles, pendants with pentagrams and several daggers.

Walter was starting a new job, there was a woman in his life again, and he was finally going to get off the booze and get his life in order. Van, with his run-ins with the law and playing around with Satanic cults, could screw things up for him. Walt was fed up. If his father in Welbourne would take him, that's where Van was gonna go.

Van hated the idea of leaving New York and his group, the only family he'd ever known. The last cult made a strong impression on him.

That night, the high priest stood before the group, dressed in black and holding a chalice of wine. He reminded them why they were together. They worshipped Satan, they indulged in the good life. They could have everything they ever wanted, if they stuck together. He read the 21 Satanic points from the *Black Book of Satan*. All that is great is built upon sorrow, he told them.

Van listened intently. He was leaving New York for a dried-up place called Kansas, and the Grotto would continue without him. But in this last ritual, the high priest intended to become the son of Satan. He would sacrifice Mia, the young woman he loved, and they would drink her blood. They would perform a ritual and then, as Satan's son, Osgood would open the gates of Hell, letting forth the demons that would help them procure the greatest riches of the world.

Van asked him how he'd learned such an amazing spell. "Mia has taught me extraordinary things," Fabian Osgood said. "She's given me ancient secrets and taught me how to practice *real* magic. You'll see."

A carafe of some unidentifiable beverage was passed around, and Van drank generously from the bottle. After a while, he began to feel strange. And then, the voices. Just like the voices that had plagued him since adolescence. He welcomed them. The voices made him feel safe and loved. He listened intently, knowing he was the chosen one, knowing that Perfect Power awaited him.

Osgood took a vial of green liquid from the pocket of his robe and drank it. Before Van's eyes, the priest seemed to change. Through the smoky haze of the candle-lit room, he watched the high priest with pure astonishment and delight. Shadows danced across the room, the darkness became alive, eating up every bit of lightness in the room.

Tiny things scurried through the room unseen. They giggled, scampering quickly to the darkest corners. Van's heart beat wildly, his excitement mounting.

Within moments, the high priest began suffocating. He gagged, stumbling about the room, coughing and wheezing. Finally, he fell to the floor. A moment or two passed, then Osgood stood. In the lightless room, he seemed different, dark and mysterious.

Though Van was well aware of Fabian Osgood's past, making it a point to know everyone's stories, he was still enthralled. Osgood was a known drug dealer, a trickster. He was a trained magician, and, in jail, had gotten himself out of a lot of trouble by amusing inmates with his magic tricks. But Van was still delighted. He believed he'd witnessed a transformation. He had to understand the magic that would open the gates of Hell, and how to obtain this ultimate power.

After the priest fell to the floor, Van crept up and sat next to him. He wanted to know his secrets. He felt compelled to ask him, but he knew it wasn't the right time.

He left for Kansas the next day, not knowing if the Grotto had performed the final ritual to secure the priest's place as the son of Satan, and if they'd actually sacrificed Mia to accomplish that goal.

All he knew was that he'd gained new knowledge from the Grotto he was leaving behind. And he intended to use it in Welbourne.

The Sheriff gripped the journal, his knuckles turning white. Skipping ahead, the last entry in Van's diary made his blood go cold.

# Chapter
## 39

Today is Walpurgisnacht, a day of lust and indulgence. This is the perfect holiday for what I've been planning. I have everything I need. Now I have to convince Melody to come with me to the altar tonight. Even though I scared her pretty bad the last time we were together, I still don't think it'll be hard. Anyway, she's in love with me. I could see it in her face when we kissed.

If this was another time and place, maybe things could have worked out for us. She surprised me. I thought being a witch, she'd have to be evil. But she has a giant heart. (I <u>saw</u> it that day at Ashby Dumping!) There've been times I wondered what it'd be like if she were really my girlfriend. She makes me feel good. And I know she really cares about me. In fact, those are some of the very reasons I've chosen her.

At any rate, I can't stop what I've started. I'm so close. Things have already happened, things I can't take back. Everything is in motion and I have to see it to the end. I'm like Abraham in the Biblical story, ready to sacrifice what he loves most. For him, his son; for me, Melody. I wonder how I will feel? Will I feel bad? Or will I feel a great strength from killing someone I care for? I can only imagine what it will be like to cut her throat. Satan will appreciate the irony. And I will open the gates to Hell, collect my minions, and take my rightful place as Satan's son.

I still don't know why High Priest Osgood never completed the ancient incantation, why he never sacrificed anyone. He could have had such power. He let his feelings for Mia weaken him. But maybe that was meant to be. I was the one to hear the voices. I've seen Satan's minions and I was chosen. At least he was willing to give me the potion when I went back to New York. Of course it took a little convincing! He told me to deny myself nothing, so taking the ancient spell was just my way of following our Satanic principles. After I've opened the gates of Hell, the secret will die with me.

My father won't be here to see my glorious victory tonight. The old man will take his place. He'll represent the earthly father I no longer lay claim to. Now it's time to go. I'm on my way to destiny, for I walk in the path of Satan. Hail Lucifer! Hail The Self!

Van Masterson, April 3Ø

# Chapter

## 40

Sheriff Larkin put out an APB out on Van Masterson. He called his Deputy Sheriff and they discussed places where Van's altar might have been erected. The first and most logical place, they decided, was Welbourne Cemetery. The Sheriff was on his way there now.

The second call was to Leotie Blackstone. He hoped that Melody would be safe at home, and that what he'd read in Van Masterson's diary was some kind of teenage fantasy. But, he doubted it. Larkin was now of the opinion that Van was a highly disturbed teenager, dangerous, and capable of committing atrocities.

Leotie answered the phone on the second ring.

"Mrs. Blackstone, this is Sheriff Larkin."

"Yes?" At the sound of his voice, terror gripped Leotie. She had to sit down.

"Is Melody home tonight?"

"No, she's not here right now," Leotie said, jumbling her words altogether. "We thought she went to the family altar. But Earl went out to get her for dinner, and she wasn't there. Is something wrong, Sheriff?"

"There may be," Sheriff Larkin paused, trying to choose words carefully. Leotie was already alarmed, and he didn't want to send her into a panic. "I have reason to believe that Van Masterson may want to harm your daughter, Mrs. Blackstone. I've just come from his house. He's not there. His grandfather isn't either, for that matter. I was hoping Melody would be home, but now I'm concerned that she may be with him. Do you know where they might have gone?"

"No! I have no idea where they would be!" Leotie's voice was shrill, near hysterical.

"Mrs. Blackstone, please try to stay calm. There's no need to panic. I'm on my way to Welbourne Cemetery, I'm hoping I might find them there. Does she have any friends who might know where Van hangs out? There might be some type of Satanic altar at this place."

"Oh, no!" Leotie cried. "She's in trouble, isn't she?" She began sobbing.

"I hope not. But here's what I want you to do. Call Melody's friends, anyone you think might be able to tell you where she and Van might be. If you find out anything, call my office and talk to Lori. She'll contact me and my Deputy."

Leotie called Bevin. Earl stood next to her. "Bevin?" Leotie sniffled into the phone.

"Who's this?" Bevin asked.

"It's Mrs. Blackstone. I have to ask you a few questions about Melody. We're worried that she may be in some danger."

"Oh my God!" Bevin gasped. "What's wrong?"

"She may be with Van Masterson, and the Sheriff thinks he wants to hurt her. Bevin, I need you to tell me if you have any idea where they might be."

Bevin bit her lower lip and closed her eyes, trying to focus on what little she knew of Van Masterson. "Okay," she said. "Let me think. They didn't go anywhere special together that I know of — mainly just The Piggy."

"Van's into some ritualistic things — Satanic worship — things of that nature," Leotie told her. "Wherever he's taken Melody — "

Bevin snapped to attention. "Ashby Dumping!" she announced.

Leotie's eyes grew wide, remembering how Melody had told her she'd seen animal sacrifices performed there.

"A few weeks ago, when we were at The Piggy, Melody said she'd seen Rudy Nobel cut the head off a chicken at Ashby Dumping. She was pretty upset about it. Anyway, Van Masterson came in and sat with us for a while, and we told him about it. He said he wouldn't mind having a look around there."

"Thank you Bevin!" Leotie hung up the phone. Time was running out and she could only imagine what Van Masterson had in store for her daughter. "She may be at Ashby Dumping," she said, looking up at Earl with blood-shot eyes.

He nodded. "'Course. Makes sense, now," he said, wearily. As though it were yesterday, he remembered a forbidden spell he'd done there with the senior Van Masterson over sixty years ago.

Leotie picked up the phone and dialed the Sheriff's office. After six rings, a girl with a soft, high voice finally picked up. "Hullo? Sheriff's office."

"Hello, Lori, this is Leotie Blackstone." There was no response on the other line. "The Sheriff told me to call you at his office when I found something out about my daughter?" Still, the girl was silent. "We think she may be at Ashby Dumping."

"Awright..." the girl said.

"So, could you call the Sheriff and Deputy immediately and let them know?"

"Awright. Who is this again?" the girl asked. Leotie was sure she could hear her smacking gum in her mouth.

"Leotie Blackstone."

"Oh! Well, okay. I'll do that, then."

"Thank you. And let him know I'm going there myself."

When Leotie hung up, Lori Greggor punched the second line on her phone, where her boyfriend had been holding. "Hang on a sec, hon, I gotta do somethin'." She made a kissy sound on the phone and put him back on hold. Then she took out her pink phone call pad and wrote: *Leotie Blackstone called and said her daughter was at Ashby Dumping. She's going there, too.* She ripped off the message, walked into the Sheriff's wood-paneled office and left the note on his cluttered mahogany desk.

Leotie hung up the phone, grabbed her keys and purse and raced for the door. Earl was on her heels. "What are you doing?" she asked.

"Coming with you," he said flatly.

"You can't. You have to stay here, in case — "

"No. I'm coming with you, Leotie. You don't know what you're heading into, and you may need me," he said.

"I don't know," she said, her voice quivering.

Earl stared at her a moment. "Leotie, I need to be there," he said. "I'm an old witch. Sometimes we just know things."

# Chapter
## 41

The Sheriff pulled into the entrance of Welbourne Cemetery. His headlights shone across the wrought-iron gate, illuminating an old man in a dingy shirt and baggy jeans that hung formless on his skinny body. The blue lights from the Sheriff's patrol car flashed across his sleepy face. Larkin got out of the car and approached the man.

"Got here as soon as I could, Sheriff. Here's the key," the groundskeeper said.

He thanked the man, who lingered after letting him through the gate. Taking out his flashlight, he flicked it on, aiming it across the cemetery. The light illuminated the graves, casting eerie shadows in the night.

Tiny, bright eyes were caught in the flashlight's beam. For a moment a rabbit stood shivering, too frightened to move. Then suddenly, it took off, leaping and darting back to the safety of the darkness.

"Let me ask you something," the Sheriff said. "Have you seen any type of altar or shrine, or, for that matter, anything unusual in the cemetery lately?"

"Altar?" The groundskeeper shook his head. "Nope. Ain't seen nothing like that in my cemetery. But they's been kids here spray-paintin' tombstones again. Little vandals! I called the Deputy a while back."

The Sheriff combed the area. He listened for voices or noises, but heard nothing. Just the occasional hooting of an owl. The cemetery was quiet and calm. He had the distinct feeling that, except for whatever restless spirits might be about, they were completely alone.

The Sheriff turned to the groundskeeper, close at his heels.

"Have you seen any of those kids in the graveyard lately?" he asked, continuing to walk briskly ahead, searching the area with his flashlight.

The groundskeeper shook his head. "Not lately."

"But you've seen them here before?"

"Yeah, I've seen some teenagers come through here, sure. Like when I seen that tall black boy with that young girl — the one screamin' 'bout diggin' up graves. Sometimes I try to tell 'em off when I see 'em, but they don't listen. I shoulda said somethin' that night, then maybe he wouldn't have dug up them graves."

"So, they go to the other side of the cemetery, over where the two graves were vandalized?"

"Yup. That's where those ones go. They come up from the west side of the graveyard, you know — by the tracks. See, there ain't no gate up that aways, so they can just walk right in. I told them to take their beers and get home, but they don't listen, Sheriff."

"Let's go over to the west side, then," the Sheriff said, and let the groundskeeper led the way.

# Chapter
## 42

Melody pulled her sweater tightly across her chest. As the sun went down, the temperature dropped several degrees, making her shiver. Feeling her tremble, Van smiled, squeezing her hand tightly.

They were headed for Ashby Dumping. Melody couldn't shake the apprehension that was sinking deep into her bones. More than a dozen times along the way, her body shuddered. She wanted to think it was from the chill in the evening air, but her intuition was screaming that something was very wrong.

"We can't stay for long," she reminded him.

Van put his arm around her and gave her a quick hug. His response warmed Melody, propelling her forward.

The crickets were especially loud at the dump site. Enjoying the hundreds of crevices the refuse heaps offered as shelter, the small bugs rubbed their wings together, singing happily into the night.

Van and Melody sat at the picnic table and were quiet for a moment, listening to the crickets and spring peepers, and watching the fireflies brighten tiny spaces in the blackness.

"Wait here," Van said and went into the small metal shed. He was back in a moment, carrying a large black duffel bag.

"What's in there?" Melody asked.

From the bag, Van procured a bottle of red wine and two glasses. He took out a corkscrew, and like a waiter at a fine restaurant, pulled the cork easily from the bottle. He poured two glasses, holding one out to Melody.

She didn't say anything.

"It's a Merlot," he explained. "Very nice wine."

"I don't drink," she said waving the glass away with her hand.

Van laughed. "I don't either. But it's a holiday. I don't think once or twice a year counts, do you?"

Melody thought of the few occasions when she, her mother, and grandfather shared a small amount of wine during the Winter Solstice celebration.

"Well, I guess not. Just a little, though."

They clinked glasses together and Van made a toast.

"Melody, you're the most intriguing girl I've ever met. You're passionate and spirited. It will be a pleasure knowing you 'til the end."

Melody shivered again. They clinked glasses and drank their wine in silence. After one glass, Melody felt her shoulders relax, the numbing effect of the alcohol beginning to take effect.

He poured her another glass of wine and she protested. "Really," she said. "That's enough. I told you, I can't stay long."

"One more glass and we'll go," he promised. Melody thought she heard an edge to his voice.

She took one sip from her glass and put it on the picnic table. Van began rummaging through his duffel bag again.

"What else do you have in there?" she teased. "You must have planned this whole thing."

"I did," he said, grinning. "Here, put this on."

Van handed Melody a long hooded black cape. She held it for a moment in her hands. It was made of soft cotton, and she could smell the faint odor of smoke on it.

"You're cold, aren't you? Go ahead, put it on," he insisted.

Melody put on the cape and had to admit, she felt more comfortable. "How do I look?" she asked, laughing giddily. The wine had relaxed her somewhat, lowering her defenses.

"Perfect. There's something I want to do now," Van said.

"Oh?"

"It may seem kind of silly, but it's symbolic. Especially for tonight, a holiday that symbolizes the unity of man and woman."

Melody pulled the cape closer to her. She waited anxiously, wanting to hear what Van was about to propose.

"When you were a kid, did you ever become blood sisters with your best friend?"

"What do you mean?"

"You know, when you prick each others fingers, then rub the blood together and promise to be friends forever?"

Melody shook her head. "That's what you want to do, become blood buddies?"

"Yeah, sort of. It's like a pact, a commitment to each other."

"Really? A commitment?" She thought for a moment. "Okay. I guess," she said with a shrug. "But then I *really* have to go."

"Give me your hand," Van said. Melody stood and turned away from him, in a teasing fashion. Finally she removed her hand from beneath her cape and held it out for Van to inspect.

He held her hand gently, examining it and stroking the soft flesh.

She giggled, enjoying his caresses. But when Van Masterson pulled out a long dagger, a scream ripped from her throat.

# Chapter
## 43

From inside the shed, Melody's scream reverberated against the metal walls. Rudy nodded at Neil and Stacey. "It's time for our big entrance," he said excitedly.

"What do we do with him?" Neil asked, pointing to Van's grandfather. His arms were tied behind his back with rope, his legs bound with wire. Duct tape held his mouth shut. He was dressed in a thin white T-shirt and overalls, and was laying on his side, shivering from the cold.

Rudy walked over to the old man and ripped the duct tape off his mouth. "Drag him out there," he ordered Neil. "This is it, man. Showtime!"

Stacey looked nervously from Rudy to Neil and then to the helpless old man lying on the floor of the cold shed. His eyes were wide with fright and he looked pleadingly at her. She could hear him mumbling. She hoped this night would go quickly, and that whatever Van had planned wouldn't involve harming anyone. But, deep inside, she pretty much knew Van had no intentions of letting either his grandfather or Melody Blackstone walk away from the evening's festivities. They'd probably never see the light of day again.

She felt sick and wondered if she might vomit. This wasn't what she'd wanted. Nobody ever told her they'd be kidnapping people. She picked nervously at the black polish on her thumbnail and gnawed on her lip. She was considering leaving, making a run for the railroad tracks. If she could make it to Welbourne

Cemetery she could hide there until everyone went home. Or maybe she could just hide in the shed until it was all over.

Neil walked over to the elder Van Masterson and grabbed hold of his feet. "Hold on," he said and began dragging him across the floor of the shed. Van groaned, as his bald head scraped the floor and bumped along the uneven surfaces.

"Come on Rudy," Neil said. "Get the other end. He's heavy you know."

Rudy was laughing. "I know exactly how much this guy weighs." He lifted old man Masterson's head and looked into his frightened eyes. "Don't worry, this will all be over soon," he said, mocking a soothing tone. Then to Stacey, "Let's go, Elvira."

Stacey rubbed her face, smudging her blood-red lipstick. Like the others, she was dressed in black with heavily caked-on makeup.

"Come on!" Rudy yelled at her. Stacey hesitated, ready to bolt. She decided she'd go outside for awhile. Maybe she'd find a better time to run like when the others were involved in the ceremony. She followed behind Rudy. It was already dark outside.

It was Van who'd kidnapped his grandfather. Well, all of them helped, but Van was the one who'd wrestled him to the floor and tied him up. Then Rudy had carried him all the way from his house to the shed, a good three-mile hike.

They were fortunate no one had seen them. It was broad daylight when they did it, and they were dressed like vampires. But, as usual, the back roads were deserted. Luck — or maybe it was the Devil — was on their side.

Once they got out to the fields by the tracks, they were in the clear. No one was ever out there. No one, it seemed, ever went into Welbourne Cemetery. And Ashby Dumping was *their* turf.

They waited for over an hour for Van to arrive with Melody. They didn't know how he was going to get her there, or what he intended to do with her. He'd ordered them to stay in the shed.

He told them when they heard screaming, they'd know it was time to come out.

Meanwhile, the three teenagers waited and drank beer. Rudy taunted Stacey, and Stacey scoffed at him. Neil sat passively, occasionally laughing at the insults that flew back and forth.

By the time Van returned, Rudy and Neil were eager to get out of the shed and let the fun begin. Stacey, on the other hand, was more worried than ever. She felt sorry for the old man. Secretly, she would have liked to help him, but she was terrified of what Van might do to her if she backed out. After all, he'd battered and bound his own grandfather!

As Stacey left the shed, she saw Van trying to tie Melody's hands behind her back. Melody was still screaming and was bleeding from her hand. She was putting up a good fight. She kicked, punched, swiped with sharp nails. Van had quite a few bloody scratches on his face.

"Stop it! Knock it off, or I'm going to have to get violent!" Van yelled, still trying to grab her other hand.

"Get away!" Melody screamed wildly. She looked terrified and furious. "Let go of me! I knew you were crazy!"

Rudy and Neil immediately went to Van's aid, grabbing Melody's free hand and yanking it behind her, practically lifting her off the ground at the same time. They bound her hands tightly. "No," Melody whimpered, suddenly aware that she was defeated.

From where he sat in the dirt by the shed, Van's grandfather shouted angrily. "For God's sake, let her go! What do ya think you're doing, boy?"

"For *God's* sake!" Van sneered. "Trust me. *He* has nothing to do with this!"

"What do you want with me? I thought you liked me!" Melody cried. Tears welled up in her eyes. Her throat tightened from fear and the strong urge to sob.

Stacey watched her, panic rising in her chest. "Yeah, what *do* you want with her, Van," she asked, and immediately regretted it.

Van turned on her. His eyes grew large with anger. His lips pulled back, exposing his teeth. He took his time answering, moving closer to her. With each slow step, Stacey's urge to run increased. He came uncomfortably close, putting his face up next to hers. She could feel the warmth of his breath on her face. For a moment, she thought he might kiss her. Looking into his baleful eyes, Stacey thought that Melody was right. Van Masterson was crazy.

He snickered. "*She*," he said, waving a hand at Melody. "She is my key to the gates of Hell. Don't you want to be there when they open, and Lucifer walks through to greet us, to offer us, his soldiers, all the earthly riches we desire? Don't you want to see him embrace me, and make me his son?"

Stacey's mouth opened large enough to accept flies. She didn't know how to respond. She tried to remember why she ever got involved in all this. How did she had let herself get this far? At one time, being around Van was fun and interesting. She'd felt privileged to be around him. He was sexy, intriguing. She felt like she belonged, that she was a part of something important. But she could see now it wasn't about being in a group. This was all about Van. It probably had been that way from the very start.

She glanced over Van's shoulder at Melody, whose jaw was trembling. Stacey could tell she was trying hard not to cry.

She shrugged. "Can we get on with it?" she said casually.

Van peered at her and Stacey held her breath, waiting to see what he'd do. He turned away.

Earlier in the day, Van had cleared away an area and built a pyre out of large branches, sticks, planks, cardboard and combustible debris from the dump. Now he poured gasoline on the heap of flammable trash and struck a match. In an instant, a roaring bonfire erupted, flames leaping high into the night, brightening the entire area of the dump.

Van went about his business without talking, gathering items from his black duffel bag and placing them together near the fire. Stacey recognized some of the objects she'd been instructed to procure for him — dead beetles, cockroaches and a variety of other bugs, several vials of human blood that Rudy had stolen from the school's Red Cross blood drive, a jar of dirt from a grave at Welbourne cemetery, animal innards, and a variety of other strange, disgusting, and obscure items.

She assumed that he had some type of incantation in mind. She remembered the day Van had relaxed them with his stupid hypnosis. They were all so eager to be in his company. She felt foolish for those feelings now.

Melody let out a shriek and skittered back on her rear, her hands still bound behind her, terrified Van was about to toss her into the fire and her burn alive.

Van's grandfather called out, "You can stop this now. There ain't no reason to do this, boy. This is just craziness. What would your father think?"

Van looked up from his work, sorting through all of the items. "That's what you're here for, old man," he said. "You're gonna tell him all about it. You're gonna let him know that I reject him as my father and you'll tell him how Satan made me his son. Once you do that, I won't need you anymore."

The words hung heavy in the air. The senior Van Masterson shrank back, looking older and more frail. "What made you this way?" he asked, sadness in his voice.

Van laughed. He turned, having finished displaying all the unusual items for the spell. He took out a document from his duffel bag and marched over to where Melody was sitting.

"Here," he said, shoving the paper in front of her.

"What's that?" she asked.

"A pact with the Devil," he said casually. "You need to sign it."

"And how am I supposed to do that?"

"Good point," Van said. He reached behind her and grabbed hold of the hand he'd slashed. He had meant to cut her wrist, but she'd moved too quickly. Getting her blood on his thumb, he wiped it onto her lips.

Melody cringed. "What are you doing?" she screeched.

Van took the document and pressed it up to her lips.

"The rest of us were able to sign it in blood. I guess a kiss in blood will be good enough," he said and walked away.

Rudy was fidgeting, biting his thumbnail. As usual, things weren't happening fast enough for him. "What do you want us to do?" he asked Van.

"There are two beams of wood by the side of the shed," he said. "There's also a hammer and some nails. I want you to nail them together, make it real strong. It should look like a cross. Get it?"

Rudy smiled. "I got it." He slapped Neil's back and the two went off to accomplish their task.

Stacey sat down at the picnic bench. Melody was only a few feet away from her, struggling hopelessly with her bindings. She noticed that the old man was watching her. His eyes beseeched her, and she knew he wanted her to help him.

She wanted to turn to him and tell him to stop looking at her that way. Even if she could untie him without being detected, he'd be of no help to her. Van had a large knife, and Stacey was certain he would use it.

"You can make do something constructive, too, Stacey," Van said. "How good are you at following directions?"

Stacey shrugged. "Fine, I guess." Van waved for her to come over to him and reluctantly, she obeyed. He handed her a yellowed piece of parchment.

"I need you to read the instructions on this paper to me while I put everything together," he said.

Stacey looked down at the paper. It was split down the middle by a line drawn in black ink. On the left half was Chinese script, on the right was English, but the language was archaic and difficult to understand.

"This looks like it's real old," Stacey commented.

"That's because it *is* old," Van said.

"Where'd ya get it?"

"Fabian Osgood," he said with pride. "The masterful high priest of the Grotto I belonged to in New York. He was a little reluctant to give it to me, but I convinced him it was the right thing to do."

Van smirked. Stacey glared at him, realizing what he really meant.

"You beat him up?"

"I prefer to think I encouraged him."

The parchment was stiff, the ink faded. Stacey worried it would crumble and turn to dust in her hands. She thought it should be in a museum someplace, not in the hands of a grungy teenager in Welbourne, Kansas.

"Don't look so upset. I *earned* it," Van said proudly. I was meant to have it. Now go on and read."

# Chapter
## 44

When Neil and Rudy were finished with the cross, they dragged it over by the bonfire. Melody stared at it wildly. She sat in the dirt, struggling with the rope tied to her wrists, which only made the knots tighten more. Her arms and hands were sore, her wrists numb.

Every now and then, she glanced over at Van's grandfather. "You're not really sick, are you?" she asked.

"Sick?"

"Van told me you were sick."

"No. Just old," he said with a huff. "Why would he tell ya that?"

"I don't know. Maybe to get close to me. He thinks he needs me — you know, for all this," she said eyeing the ritualistic nonsense around her.

"Well, he's a *liar*," the grandfather said, flatly.

Melody swallowed hard. She remembered all the amazing stories he'd told her about himself. She felt stupid. Everything he'd said had been a lie.

They were silent for a moment. Stacey was standing ten yards away with Van, trying desperately to make sense of the old spell. Neil and Rudy were digging a hole in the ground near the fire.

"He's going to let you go," Melody said, offering the old man a weak smile.

He frowned. "Don't think so."

"Do you think he really wants to... *kill* me?" she sputtered, her eyes wide with fear.

"*No!* No, I don't think he'd do anythin' like that!" he said, not sounding too convincing. His lips trembled. "I'm sorry," he said, a hitch in his voice. "I'm sorry I didn't stop this sooner. I knew my grandson weren't right. He's had problems, ya know. Psychological things.

"I went to see your granddaddy, after I found all that devil stuff in my house." He paused, closing his eyes tightly. A tear escaped his closed lids. "Oh, God," he moaned. "First your daddy... now you."

"My dad?" Melody asked, confused. "What do you mean?" Masterson went on talking to himself. "I wanted to love my grandson," he said, choking on the words. "I wanted to do right by him. I don't think he felt like he was much loved."

Melody heard Van shouting at Stacey. "What's wrong with you? Can't you read English? Just open your mouth and read the words. How hard is that?"

"But it doesn't make any sense, Van! It's worse than reading Shakespeare!" Stacey screamed back.

They shouted back and forth. Suddenly furious, and sick of all the games and threats, Stacey tossed the ancient parchment. It lifted, floating above their heads like a leaf in the wind. Abruptly, a current of air caught the paper and pulled it toward the bonfire.

In a panic, Van leapt after it. He touched the edges of the paper with his fingers, but it moved past him, dragged right into the fire.

"NO!" Van bellowed. A red-orange tongue of fire licked at the parchment, dissolving it quickly into ash.

Van whipped around, fury in his eyes. Seeing his rage, Stacey turned to run, but Van was on her. He tackled her to the ground, and pinned her hands up over her head.

"You stupid girl!" he screamed. "Do you know how valuable that was? It was an ancient spell!" he shrieked, spit sprayed from his mouth onto her face.

Stacey screeched.

Rudy chuckled coming towards them. "Stacey. You did a very bad thing," he said, waving a finger at her.

"Whoa!" Neil said, throwing his shovel down. He ran over crying, "Hang on, Van, she didn't mean it! Come on, leave her alone."

Neil grabbed Van by the shoulders and tried yanking him off Stacey.

"Don't!" Van said, whipping his head around. "Don't *ever touch me*! Nobody *ever* touches me *again*!" He shook off Neil's hands and pulled the dagger from its holster in his belt. He pointed the blade towards Neil who quickly backed away.

Neil looked from Van to Stacey. For once, she wasn't the cool, tough girl she usually seemed to be. Defenseless and scared, she looked up at Neil.

Anger rose in Neil at the thought of anyone hurting her. "Back off, Van!" he hollered, stepping forward. "Stacey doesn't deserve to be treated like this!" For a moment, the thought of actually fighting Van flickered through Neil's mind.

"I didn't mean to lose your damn paper," Stacey snapped, sitting up.

Neil looked from Van to Stacey. Did she really need his help, after all?

Van sheathed the knife. "Get up," he ordered and Stacey scurried back towards the shed.

Van went back to where he'd carefully laid out all the items for his incantation. He looked frantically at the assortment, shaking his head. How would he know what to do with it all — how it should all go together? How would he know what words to speak?

"Wasted!" he cried in rage. "It's all a waste! Everything I did to get here!"

He'd worked so hard on the preparations, set everything in motion. He'd done his animal sacrifices, kidnapped his grandfather and Melody. What if he wasn't able to make it happen? What was he going to do? Without the spell, it was useless.

He closed his eyes tight, pressing the palms of his hands to his forehead. There had to be a way to summon the Devil, to bring forth his minions without the spell. If he only knew someone who could remember the spell by heart. He thought of Osgood. That was pointless. Things were unraveling.

Then he heard something scampering through the dusty earth. Giggling from some hidden corner of the overflowing, filthy dump. The voices whispered deep and low. "*Invoke the voice of Satan, and you will be heard. Perfect power is yours.*"

Horrified, Melody watched as Van searched the ground for the little imps they both had heard. Her entire body trembled. Like lightening, fast and radiant across a dull sky, she was suddenly illuminated with insight.

At once she understood what had been happening. She remembered her visions — the prowler's hands digging in the earth, the tracker chasing the cat. All along, it had been Van.

She'd been hearing what *he* heard — seeing what *he* saw. His twisted mind had created horrible little black imps. And somehow, she was linked to him.

A small cry fell from her lips. She'd misused magic and the tools of Wicca, and somehow she'd opened a door that let Van and his creatures into her life. Suddenly, she remembered the dream she'd had of her father. "You have brought forth the very thing you sought," he'd told her.

She realized that the only time she'd communicated with her father was when *he* reached out to her. Now she understood what her mother had tried to tell her: that if he needed to, he'd find a way to contact her. She couldn't force the universe to give her what she wanted against its lawful rules anymore than Van could in his way.

Melody watched as Van stomped back over to his gym bag and pulled out another vial of the green-blue liquid. "Remember this?" He teased Melody, holding up the glass container.

"Think logically for a second," Melody stammered. "That stuff doesn't make you powerful, Van, it just makes you..."

"Crazy?" he finished. "No it doesn't make me crazy, Melody. It makes me a god. With this," he said holding up the vial, "I am one of Satan's own, with all the powers and privileges that go with that. I have the memory of a hundred devils and the experience of a thousand lifetimes. In this state, I understand things. I see *through* people, understand *everything* about them! It gives me the power to open the gates of Hell. I don't need a spell," he huffed. "But of course, I do need *you*, witch-girl! After I sacrifice you, the world, in its totality, is mine."

Melody closed her eyes. When she opened them again, Van was staring at her. She startled at the softness in his blue eyes. Was the old Van back again?

"Anything is better than what I am right now," he whispered, then tilted his head back and poured the liquid down his throat.

# Chapter

Leotie's heart was racing. "Please let her be alright," she prayed. She was following Earl, who seemed to know the way to Ashby Dumping as if he'd been there yesterday. The man never ceased to amaze her. Though he had a few infirmities, he was a rugged man for seventy-six.

They'd taken the shortcut, following the railroad tracks that cut through the wheat and alfalfa fields. Leotie knew of the dump's hazards and had forbidden her daughter to go there. It was a deserted, filthy piece of earth that became more dangerous as the years went by. As far as Leotie knew, it wasn't even a legal dumping place. As she hurried along the tracks, she prayed that the Sheriff had got her message.

The night was especially black with clouds that covered any chance of moonlight. Without the aide of a flashlight, Leotie and Earl fumbled as they tried to cover distance as quickly as they could. Once, Earl lurched, almost falling. Leotie grabbed him by the arm, quickly righting him. Then, she stumbled and painfully twisted her ankle. She tried to keep her mind clear, pushing away negative thoughts. She also tried to strategize.

It was possible that Van Masterson had a gun or some other weapon. She kicked herself for not bringing her daddy's Winchester double-barrel shotgun. It was old, but it still worked fine. It could blast a hole through the side of a barn. No flashlight, no shotgun — she should have been more prepared.

Now she tried to imagine what she would do if Van was armed. Maybe she could talk to him, coax him out of whatever he was threatening to do. She was prepared to do anything to rescue her daughter.

For a moment, the moon, bright and full, came out from behind a cloud. It illuminated the path they were on, and they could see the clearing up ahead. Earl immediately recognized the back entrance to Ashby Dumping.

They saw the bonfire first, its blaze a shrine to the darkness. It crackled and spit as it roasted the wood and debris in its center. Leotie looked around wildly, trying to locate Melody. Her eyes darted across several teenagers dressed in black, like vampires out for a night's feeding. Her eyes fell across old man Masterson. He was tied up and bleeding from his head, but seemed otherwise unharmed. Finally her eyes came to rest on Melody. She was alive! She was tied and sitting in the dirt.

Fueled by pure adrenaline, Leotie pushed her way past a black-clad teenager and hurdled over the bound old man. Someone tried to grab her around the waist, but she ripped their hands away, flying towards her daughter.

Melody screamed, "Mom!" — not a cry for help, but a warning. It was too late. Leotie was down, the wind knocked out of her lungs. Struggling to breathe, her mind reeled, wondering what had happened.

Finally, air filled her lungs and she inhaled. She opened her eyes to find herself staring into the baleful eyes of Van Masterson. He was giggling, low and menacing. "You're nothing but a glowing ember," he chuckled, looking at her with *new* vision. "Burning, that's what you are," he said, rising. "Anger, love, passion. It makes you burn!" He tipped his head back and laughed uproariously. Leotie could see he was demented, or drugged, or both.

She sat up, ready to pitch her body at him, then recoiled. He pointed a large, sharp dagger at her face. It swung back and forth as Van snickered and muttered.

Melody watched him from where she sat, still held powerless by the ropes that bound her. Van had the same bizarre expression on his face as the day they were together at Ashby Dumping.

A tall black boy, one of the teens, was laughing hysterically.

"Don't hurt her!" the scraggly voice of Van's grandfather pleaded. "She's a *mother*, for Christ's sake. Ain't no reason to hurt her. And Melody's just a child. Take me, but please leave the others. I'm beggin' ya."

The fire was roaring and the air was filled with its smoky smell.

"Yeah, she's a *mother*," Van said, mockingly. "And what good are they really, anyway? What the hell do they do for you? Because," he said, looking directly at Melody, "you never know when they're gonna desert you." He smiled. "Or die! In fact," he said, an edge to his voice, "what better way to venerate Satan than to sacrifice the mother of a witch? Two witches for the price of one. What a yard sale!"

Earl Blackstone stood at the edge of Ashby Dumping, fists clenched, his face stern. He watched Van's restless movements, as he darted this way and that, moving about the barren earth, looking confused. The boy wanted to believe in himself, wanted others to believe in him. But Earl could see that the truth was, he was uncertain, insecure. Earl waited, because sometimes it was best just to wait.

"Untie Melody," Van said, standing. His dagger was still positioned at Leotie's face, its razor-sharp point touching her cheek.

Although he'd heard the command, Rudy asked, "What?"

"I said, untie her!" Van roared. "Use the ropes to tie her mother."

Rudy began untying Melody. She kicked at him and spit in his face. "Do whatever you want," he said smirking. "But you're still the lamb going to the slaughter." He smiled wickedly.

Still holding onto Melody by the wrist, Rudy tossed the ropes to Neil. He stood, taking the cord. Hesitating, he looked over at Melody's mother, wondering what to do. He wanted out of this now, things were out of hand. He took a step and stopped.

"Hey! Tie her up," Rudy yelled. When Neil continued to delay, Rudy yanked Melody over to Neil and took the ropes back. "Here, hold onto her, then," he said, pushing Melody into Neil. Rudy stormed over to Leotie, bent down, grabbed her roughly and began binding her hands behind her back. When he was done, he asked Van, "Now what?"

"There's wire in the shed," Van told Rudy. "Get it. Tie Melody to the cross with it."

"No!" Melody screamed. With a savage strength borne of sheer terror, she punched Neil squarely in the nose. To both their surprise, his nose popped, spraying blood across their faces.

"My nose!" he hollered. "You busted it!" He put his hands up to his face, cradling his broken nose protectively. Melody ran for the shed.

"Leave her alone!" Leotie screamed at Rudy as he took off after her, liking the exciting twist this game was taking.

"I still have your *mother*," Van yelled to his fleeing prey. His voice sang out the word "mother," teasing her like a mean adolescent holding an ice cream cone over a three-year old's head. Then he glimpsed old Earl Blackstone, who stood, still frozen in his tracks, at the edge of the dump. Van chuckled to himself. The old guy's paralyzed with fright. "And your grandfather for that matter! I'd get back here if I were you!" he said, laughing.

Melody hesitated, then obeyed, inching her way back towards the fire, her eyes locked carefully on Van. Rudy moved in quickly, pulling her back towards the wooden cross. Pushing her down, he pinned her to the cross with all his body weight, and then tightly bound her feet and hands. She screamed as the wire cut into her flesh, her already wounded hand throbbing with pain.

Neil still hadn't moved. His head was tipped back, blood smeared across his face, mixing with the black and white makeup. "I think it's broken," he whimpered as Van brushed by him, towards Leotie.

Leotie had moved herself into a kneeling position. She could hear herself screaming. As Van approached, she gave a guttural, low growl, like an angry caged animal.

"I forgot to welcome you to my lair, dear mother," Van said with thick sarcasm, the timbre of his voice eerie and low.

Leotie watched him run his tongue across his teeth, as though sharpening them for a feast. "You're an unexpected guest," he said. "But I'm delighted at the turn of events."

"What do you think you're *doing*?" Leotie barked. She'd yet to figure out how she was going to stop Van Masterson, but she knew she would. She had to.

"What I was destined to do. I am a servant of Satan, a soldier who will inherit great riches, and I will live a thousand lifetimes."

Leotie shuddered, realizing Van actually believed what he was saying.

With Melody shrieking in his ears, Rudy began pulling the cross up. Van turned around to look. "I want it upside-down," he said.

"What?" Rudy asked, perplexed.

"Turn the cross the other way, so that her head is down, and plant it in the hole in the ground," he ordered.

Leotie painfully hopped to her feet. Horrified, she watched as Melody, secured to the wooden cross with wire, was tipped upside-down. The girl was screaming in terror, her long sandy hair flopping all about.

Leotie stood ready to fight, but shrank back when Van brandished the dagger in her direction. She bared her teeth at him, feeling powerless. With her hands bound, and an obviously delusional boy threatening both her and her daughter's life, her mind reeled trying to find a way out.

She thought about using witchcraft. A hundred spells went through her mind — spells for protection, for knowledge, and for expelling negative vibrations — but nothing that could help the situation she was in now.

She'd devoted her life to learning the Craft. She'd been taught magic, and she'd learned to believe in her own inner powers. She acknowledged that in all human beings there is a depth of power far greater than anyone can comprehend. And, sometimes, that could only be called supernatural.

But she didn't know what magic could do if it was turned towards something evil. She'd never believed in the concept of supreme evil. She didn't believe in the Devil. In general, she thought that people were, at their core, good. She'd never before encountered someone with such evil intentions.

She closed her eyes tight and prayed silently, "*Hear me Queen of the Green Earth, and Star Goddess. I call upon you to aid me, to defeat this boy, to end this terrible evil, and save my daughter.*"

As Leotie ended her silent prayer, Van began reading from a black book. He was beseeching his own god. Leotie dropped her head. She tried to grasp the idea that if magic could work for her, then Van might be able to call upon another kind of magic.

# Chapter
## 46

Van bellowed out his prayer. "*Lucifer, we call you. We are but your lowly servants, humbled by your power and eager to serve you. Open now the gates to your world, so that we may be a part of it. Look now and see us, acting on your words, acting on your behalf. We are eager to do as you command.*"

He moved to the bonfire and spoke into its flames. "*On this sacred night of Walpurgisnacht we have sacrifices for you. A Wiccan girl and her mother are my gifts to you, our lord. We have built an inferno, a gateway to Hell, so that you might open its doors and pass through, and that you may crown me your son.*"

Melody watched Van, as she hung upside-down on the wooden cross. She was beginning to feel dizzy. All the blood in her body was rushing to her head. She was afraid she might faint.

Van closed the *Black Book of Satan* and marched over to Melody. He stood for a moment, inches away from her face, gazing into her eyes.

She stared back, unflinching. He knew she had to be afraid. But fear wasn't what he saw. Her eyes conveyed an inner courage and honesty, and he felt his ego wither under her scrutiny.

"You don't scare me, Van," Melody said. "I feel sorry for you."

He gave a raspy laugh. "And you don't fool me, Melody." He laughed again. "You and me — we're really one and the same. We're perfectly matched, perfectly alike," he told her.

"We're nothing alike," she said, scornfully. Her head throbbed. She was seeing double. She blinked, trying to focus.

"Oh no? Like me, you use magic to your own advantage. You don't care who it hurts. You're only interested in how it benefits you."

Melody cringed. Van watched her expression as it changed from boldness to chagrin.

"I've made mistakes," Melody admitted, biting a trembling lip. "But I'm spiritual. Something you know nothing about. Your only *power* is that you have the ability to convince others to join you. Otherwise," she huffed, "you're just a loser."

Van recoiled. "And you're my little lamb. But we share the same faith, the same religion."

"They're *not* the same," Melody hissed through gritted teeth.

"Oh, no? We even share the same holidays. Here it is, Walpurgisnacht. You call it Beltane. Are they not the same? A time of lust and indulgence..."

"Wiccan is an earth-based religion that predates Christianity and your Devil," Melody said. She coughed from a lack of air. "If you celebrate your rituals at the same time as our holidays, it's because *you've* stolen *our* holidays. You try to make us the same, but we share nothing. You're all alone, Van."

"You'll know what it's like to be alone when you die, Melody," he sneered. He held up his dagger, enjoying seeing the fear well up in her eyes. "A toast to Satan," he said, slashing her wrist. The blood poured quickly, and at first Melody couldn't feel her hand. Then, quite suddenly, she felt the pain rip through her body. Her shrill scream pierced the air.

Leotie bolted towards Van. He knocked her down with one swift blow to her stomach, then stepped past her. "It's time," he said. He turned to Rudy who was watching him, nervously fiddling with the tie on his black robe. "Gather the members and bring them close to the fire," Van ordered.

Rudy nodded, looking around for Neil. He spotted him at a far corner of the dump, standing silently, watching in the shadows. "Come on! Van says it's time," he said. Neil shrugged, turning his face away. "Where's Stacey?" Rudy asked. Neil didn't answer. It was clear that he was no longer interested in participating. And as Rudy scanned the area for Stacey, he realized the Grotto was down two members.

Flustered, Rudy took off in search of Stacey. He opened the door to the metal shed, looked inside, and found it empty. He rushed over to the lean-to, explored inside, even checking the roof to make sure she wasn't perched on top, hiding in the shadows. Stacey was nowhere around. Rudy made his way back to Van. "I can't find Stacey," he confessed. "And Neil..."

Van lurched forward, making Rudy jump back. "Don't worry," Van breathed. "We'll find her. And Neil — I'll find a purpose for him," he said, sneering.

Melody was woozy. She was afraid to close her eyes and yield to darkness. She was afraid if she did, she'd never open her eyes again. She looked down at her wrist and could see that it was bleeding badly.

Her mother was lying on her side, curled up in a ball on the ground. Melody wanted to call to her, to see if she was okay, but she didn't have the strength. Dread welled up in her. What if her mother was seriously hurt? What if she was dead?

Panic sucked the breath from her lungs. In an instant, she understood what was important in her life. She'd wasted so much time being angry and despondent, blaming others for her unhappiness. She'd dwelt so much on missing her father, trying to find some way to communicate with him, all the while shutting her mother out.

She'd felt sorry for herself, worrying what kids at school thought of her, when in the end, it didn't matter. It was the people she loved and cared about that mattered. It was the living that continued to affect her life. The dead could only offer memories. Seeing her mother crumpled on the ground, Melody feared these were lessons learned too late.

Perspiration trickled down her forehead and into her eyes. She blinked, then suddenly saw her grandfather moving towards her. He approached with a slight stoop.

"Gramps?" Melody whispered.

"Yup, it's me," he whispered back.

"Get out of here," she said, "or he's going to kill you, too." Suddenly a violent wave of nausea assaulted her. She closed her eyes tight.

"Quiet, now," Earl told her. From the back pocket of his faded overalls, he pulled out a small pair of pliers and began snipping at the wire around her wrists.

Melody was afraid she was going to vomit or pass out. The gash in her wrist was agonizing and now her back and head throbbed mercilessly.

Suddenly her wrists were freed. She opened her eyes. At first, her vision was blurry. She blinked several times and then brought the faces into focus. Stacey was standing next to her grandfather. Her face, heavily caked with white and black makeup, had been smudged by tears.

"Sshhh," she whispered, wrapping medical gauze tightly around Melody's wrist. "You have to be quiet. Don't move until I tell you."

Melody nodded.

"You wouldn't believe the things I keep in my bag," Stacey whispered, smiling weakly. "All sorts of things. This is the first time I've ever needed gauze. Glad it was in there."

"Where's Van?" Melody asked, looking around.

"Looking for *me*," Stacey replied, fearfully.

Stacey finished dressing Melody's wounds. "I hope that helps," she said. Melody's grandfather and Stacey pushed against the wooden cross. "Hold on," Stacey said as the cross toppled to the ground.

As she laid on the ground, her grandfather snipped snip the rest of the wire bindings around her ankles. Freed, Melody slid from the cross onto the ground, landing on her face. She coughed and shook her head.

"My mom," she whispered, her voice croaking. She pointed to her mother who was still lying in a heap on the ground.

Earl nodded. He handed the pliers to Stacey and she quickly crept to Leotie. She gently rocked her shoulders. "Are you all right?" she whispered urgently. "We have to get out of here."

Leotie gasped and opened her eyes. "Where's Melody?" she cried in a sudden outburst.

Stacey hushed her. "You have to be quiet." She quickly snipped at the ropes on Leotie's wrists. "She's over there," she pointed to Melody and Earl who were making their way toward the dump's entrance, where Van's grandfather was still tied up, lying in the dirt.

Leotie felt the ropes loosen on her wrists and eagerly yanked her hands free. She jumped to her feet, racing to her daughter. Turning Melody around, she searched her face. Melody smiled at her. "Mom, I'm so sorry!

Leotie pulled Melody into her, feeling her muffled cries against her shoulder. Tears fell from her face.

Stacey knelt beside Van's grandfather, putting the pliers to the bindings on his legs. Fearfully, she glanced around the dump, terrified Van would be back at any moment. Everything in her made her want to run away. But she didn't. She came back to help.

She also knew their time was almost up. Van would be back, and there was still a ritual to be done. People were scheduled to die.

As soon as she was finished getting the old man free, as soon as she felt the tracks beneath her feet, she would run faster than she had in her whole life.

# Chapter
# 47

Sheriff Larkin was emerging on the west side of Welbourne Cemetery when static hissed from his two-way radio.

"Sheriff?" the high pitched feminine voice called out.

"Go ahead, Lori," Larkin urged.

"Right, well…" the Sheriff waited, as he imagined Lori Greggor shifting the large wad of gum around in her mouth. "Did the Deputy Sheriff get holda ya?"

"No," Sheriff Larkin said back into the receiver. "Why, what's going on? Did Bob find Melody Blackstone?"

"Yup, well…" she paused again, the Sheriff could hear her chewing. "Her momma called earlier and the Deputy picked up the message. I did leave it on *your* desk, Sheriff," she said indignantly. "It was somethin' 'bout them bein' at Ashby Dumpin'. I dunno, but I thought he'd of called ya by now. Seemed real uptight when he left."

The Sheriff hesitated, putting the two-way radio up to his forehead. Then he clicked the receiver with his thumb again, asking, "Why's that, Lori?" There was an edge to his voice. Why hadn't Deputy Sheriff Bob Wilson called to update him?

"Ya know," Lori's little voice said, "guess it was *his* German Shepherd that them kids chopped up. Left it on his porch for him to find in the mornin'. If ya ask me, *I* think he's been waitin' to get his hands on the person responsible. Ya know, the Deputy, he's down right *mad*."

"Send two cruisers to Ashby Dumping right away, Lori. *Right away*," he emphasized. "I'm on the west side of Welbourne Cemetery, and I'm on foot. I should be there in a few minutes."

"Roger that, Sheriff," Lori's voice replied daintily. Then she popped her gum over the intercom. "Oh, Sheriff?"

"Yes?"

"He took your riffle."

# Chapter
## 48

Stacey felt Van's threatening stare even before she looked up. Still crouching over his mumbling grandfather, she slowly lifted her eyes to Van's. His blue eyes held such malice it made her shudder. She tried to remember what he'd been like before, what allure he'd held that had made her follow him so blindly.

"There you are," he said, in cheery sarcasm.

Van shook his head watching them. They'd actually thought they could sneak away, he thought with amusement. They really didn't understand the vastness of his powers.

With a swift attack, Rudy had already reclaimed their lamb for the slaughter. Leotie and Earl tried unsuccessfully to keep their grasp on Melody, but Rudy was too strong. Melody struggled, slapping Rudy uselessly on his giant back as he half dragged, half carried her to Van.

Van was enjoying feeling omnipotent. He was changing inside. Things he once cared about were fading. Thoughts of his father, the sound of honking cabs in the city, playing pool with his friends, even the taste of pizza with extra cheese and onions — it was all becoming vague memories. With every passing moment, Van lost pieces of his humanity. He was giving up his soul. Now he felt as demonic as the whispering voices in his head.

"Come on, Stacey," he ordered. "Leave the old guy alone. He's not going anywhere. We still have a ritual to get on with." He looked at Earl Blackstone, who glared back stony-faced. Van turned to Stacey. "Looks like we'll be feeding more of you to the fire than originally expected," he sneered.

Stacey stood up, looking pleadingly at Van. She scanned the dump yard. Where had Neil gone off? Did he simply leave? One attempt to help her, one gesture of good faith and then, as usual, "Oops! Things are gettin' outta control, gotta go now."

"Neil?" Stacey called into the thin night air.

Van laughed, looking around. "Do you see him here? Guess not! Oh well, Stacey. He must be gone. Did you really think your boyfriend was going to save you? Did you really think any *one* of you would be saved? Business as usual, let's go."

Van pressed his dagger firmly against Melody's throat, threatening to puncture her jugular at any moment. He tugged at her arm, trying to move her towards the bonfire. She resisted, and he yanked harder. With all her will, she pulled her body against his.

Her defiance caught Van off guard, and Melody stole the opportunity, whirling away from him back into the arms of her family. She stood next to them, resolute to die fighting.

"Huh," Van said, surprised. "So this is the way you want it?" He eyed each Blackstone member, as they tried to stare him down. Then, quick as a cat, he was on Leotie. He wrapped himself around her, pulling her into him, his dagger digging into her abdomen. Earl reached for Van, but he was like some slippery creature come up from the sewer. Earl scraped his arm across the razor-sharp blade in Van's hand, opening a gash in his weathered arm.

"This is better," Van seethed. He tightened his grip on Leotie, moving backwards. "You're just a mother," he said into her ear. "And who needs *mothers*? Time to die."

Stacey, frozen with fear, hovered over old man Masterson. She someone approaching the bonfire and her heart leapt. It was Neil, moving awkwardly. He saw her and smiled uncertainly. Warily, she smiled back.

"NO!" Melody shrieked. Stacey jumped. "Don't *touch* my mother!" she commanded.

Conditioned by years of responding to cult authority, Van hesitated, the dagger in his hand twitching. Next to him, Rudy wavered, wondering what to do as his leader faltered.

In the fashion of her family's ancient Wiccan courage, Melody confronted Van. "*See not with your eyes the visions, use your heart and intuition,*" she said, repeating her dead father's words.

The visions were back, but now they weren't confusing. She could read Van's every thought — his mind, a jumbled pile of garbage, like the filth at Ashby Dumping.

"I *know* you," Melody said, her voice steady. "You think you know people's stories, and that their little secrets give you power. But I know all *your* ugly secrets, too. You're just a sad, abandoned little boy," she said, seeing the lost kid in her mind who'd been discarded, unloved, and unwanted all his life.

Van looked confused, like a kid who showed up to trick-or-treat on the wrong night.

"The demons from your past have taken on a life of their own," she said, thinking of the little black creatures that scurried about, whispering empty promises into his psychotic mind. "I see them, too. They lie to you, those demons. Satan lies," she said. "You're giving everything up to those lying little imps. They're not giving *you* power. You're giving your power to them. *There is no perfect power!*"

Van blinked. How did she know the secret words? Did she see and hear Satan's minions, too? Was she also chosen?

Puzzled, he stood back, the dagger dangling in his hand. Then, from behind, Stacey begged, "Please. Please *let us go!*" She cried, then let loose a river of tears.

"Let you go?" Van snapped, shaken out of his trance. He gripped the dagger again, this time so tight, his knuckles turned white. "Let you go? Where to? *This* is Hell. *This* is where all your souls belong."

Van let go of Leotie and went for Stacey. He thrust the knife at Stacey's neck. She screamed, falling backwards. The dagger nicked her ear and stabbed the earth. Van pulled the knife out, held her with one hand, then plunged it through the air towards her throat.

Suddenly, Neil was on top of Van, he held his arm back mid-air, the dagger dangling in front of Stacey's horrified face. "Let go!" Neil roared and rolled Van onto his back, the dagger flying from his clutch. Neil straddled him, staring into his face. "I *believed* in you," he spat. Then he punched him Van in the face. Van hollered as the pain shot through his jaw.

The two boys began rolling on the ground, raising a cloud of dust as their fists flew. Above the sounds of their grunting and cursing, Stacey screamed, and Rudy hollered, not sure who was winning, or who he should help.

The ragged voice of Van's grandfather repeated the Lord's Prayer over and over.

Cutting through the commotion came the booming sound of a rifle. Melody felt the breeze of a bullet pass her face. As the sound of the gunshot subsided, it grew strangely quiet. The peepers and crickets stopped their chatter. No night birds called. An eerie hush fell over everything. Ashby Dumping was quiet as a morgue.

In the confusion, Van had managed to retrieve his dagger and make it over to Melody. She saw the stocky figure of the Deputy Sheriff moving towards them, his rifle aimed directly at Van's head. She felt the pinch of the dagger on her neck.

"Van Masterson," the Deputy called out. "Put your weapon down or I'm going to blow your stinkin' head off."

Melody looked at Van. Casually, he looked back, an evil smirk on his face. "Put it down, Van," she told him. "Or he'll *kill* you."

Van leaned closer, still gripping the blade. "Do you know the story of Abraham and Isaac?" he asked softly, every word distinct in the airless silence. "Like Abraham, I'm willing to sacrifice the one I love most to my god. Once you've committed yourself to doing the act, once you've raised your hand to strike down the one you love, there comes a transformation in your heart and soul. The deed is as good as done."

He pressed the cold steel deeper against her throat. Even as she heard her mother scream in terror, heard the gunshot rip through the air, and the sound of approaching police sirens, it all seemed far away to her as she said her final prayer.

*"Perfect love and perfect trust, prepare my soul to return to dust. I invoke the spirits of a higher power. Guard me and mine in this grave hour."*

The last thing Melody heard was her grandfather's voice. "Don't shoot," she heard him say. "He's unarmed."

# Chapter
## 49

When Melody opened her eyes, she was certain she was dead. Everything was blurry, noises were muffled. Was this what the afterlife looked like? But a throbbing in her wrist and an aching in her head let her know she was very much alive. A screaming ambulance brought her to her senses. She blinked, seeing her mother's face.

"It's all right, you just fainted, honey," Leotie said. "Just fainted," she repeated, as if trying to convince herself.

"What happened?" she asked. She looked up, seeing her grandfather. He helped her to a seated position.

"Your Gramps saved us all!" a raspy, old voice said.

Melody glanced up at the senior Van Masterson, who hovered over her. He rubbed his hands over and over, as if washing them with imaginary water, trying to bathe away the night's events.

Melody looked around and caught a glimpse Van being put in the back of the Sheriff's cruiser. Outside the vehicle, she could see the Sheriff talking with the Deputy. Both looked angry, but the Sheriff was definitely giving the other man a dressing down of some sort.

"What'd he do?" Melody asked, smiling wearily at her Gramps. He had a strange calm expression on his face, probably relief that the horrible nightmare had finally ended.

"I ain't never seen such a thing," old Masterson continued. "Your Gramps moved so fast, I don't even think I saw him. It was like the knife disappeared outta my grandson's hands. Jes like that," he attempted to snap his fingers, but no sound came out. "Saved ya life, he did. An' all of ours." He nodded at Earl Blackstone.

Melody looked from the senior Van Masterson to her grandfather.

"Thing is..." the old man said, running a hand across his face. Melody could see where the wire had dug into his wrinkled skin, causing deep purple bruises. "I been wantin' to tell your whole family somethin' for a long time now. Earl, you saved my grandson's life tonight. Sure as I'm standin' here, Bob Wilson woulda shot him if ya hadn't taken his knife away."

"Well, you know," Earl Blackstone drawled, "the Sheriff's warning shot really made the difference."

"Nah. It was you." Masterson said. "Ya saved my life. Ya saved my grandson." He paused. "And I wished I woulda saved your son's life."

"What do you mean?" Earl asked, the color draining from his face.

"I was there that night, Earl," Masterson's voice choked. "Damn that Patrick MacIntire. He was drunk again. I saw him from where I was sittin' in my booth. Jes came in to eat, ya know. I used to do that, on account of how lonely I'd get." His eyes were sad. "I didn't see Erik at first. Guess he was in a booth, too.

"Well, MacIntire was in a bad mood that night. Drunk again. Hittin' on his wife. Then I saw Erik tryin' to talk to him. Sweet as pie, that boy. Always tryin' to do the right thing. Tried talkin' nice to him, but the man weren't in the right frame of mind. I went to stand up, but then sat back down. 'None of my business,' I tell myself. 'Stay outta it.' Like when we was kids, Earl. Ain't that how we got in trouble? Gettin' inta other people's business?

"He was drunk," he repeated, as though it were an excuse for the violent crime that followed. "He jes picked up that bottle so fast, don't think anyone at the bar coulda stopped him.

"Ya see, MacIntire, he went to my church. I coulda talked to him. He liked me. Respected me. Least I think he did." Masterson lowered his tear-swelled eyes. "Been holdin' it in for almost two years now, Earl. I'm so sorry."

Earl Blackstone stood unmoving. Even his eyes weren't blinking. Melody thought he was going to have a heart attack, that he was going choke up, clutch his chest and simply die. The thought that her father might have been saved — that a drunken wife-beating man in a pub might have been stopped — brought blood hot and pulsating to her face. What kind of people were the Mastersons anyway? She closed her eyes, wishing the night would go away, wishing all of it would end.

Then she felt her mother gently stroking her long hair. Suddenly, she was soothed and calmed. "Providence, remember?" she said to her daughter.

Finally Earl Blackstone moved. Like the tinman in *The Wizard of Oz*, Leotie's words had oiled the mechanics of his heart.

"So, you're the one been puttin' flowers on the altar," he said to the senior Van Masterson who startled. The tears that clung to his eyeballs finally dripped down his wintry face. "How... how'd ya know it was me."

"Just a guess," Earl said. "But why?"

"Dunno. Homage, I guess. That an'... well, guess cause there's a powerful force in how we pray and worship."

Earl Blackstone smiled. "Van, who knows what ya coulda done or not done to help my son. But I'm glad ya told me the truth. Your grandson's gonna need a lot of help. Reckon he'll be needin' to see a doctor about them voices he's been hearin' and such. And, I reckon he's gonna be locked up someplace," he said. A long, deep sigh escaped his chest. "So, if ya need someone to talk to, I'll be here."

Old man Masterson smiled wearily and nodded.

Melody tried standing. Leotie wrapped an arm around her waist, lifting her up. "I think I can wait now," Melody said.

"For what?" Leotie asked.

"You know, to find Mr. Right, the man I'm destined to marry."

"Ah," Leotie said nodding.

"And I don't think I'll be needing magic to find him either."

"I think you're right."

"I guess some things are better left to wonder about." Melody smiled.

As he was getting into his cruiser, the Sheriff turned back to his Deputy, wrapping up his conversation. "I noticed that too, he said. "It was strange how silent it got there for a while. I don't think I've ever noticed a silence like that before. Everything was just dead quiet. And then I heard that thing you were talking about — that bird, or frog, or whatever it was. Like nothing I've ever heard before." He paused, then shivered. "Sounded like giggling."

# ☙THE END❧

In high school, Jennifer B. White was wicked cool, and never once had a zit. She eats cereal from the box; likes long walks on the beach—but only if pirates are chasing her; roller coasters, 'cause she loves the sensation of having to hurl; and the smell of her cat's breath. She's not afraid to check under the bed for monsters. Unless it's really dark. But, more than anything—whether it's a book or a movie—Jennifer enjoys a great story. Aside from being an awesome mom, writing a really good tale is what she lives for. That, and pumpkin pie.

She's an author, screenwriter, and Hollywood tagline writer. She lives and writes in Boston, Massachusetts, when she's not in Los Angeles, California working on movies. She holds a BA in communication and an M.Ed in psychology. She has three boys—all were born in late October, the youngest on Halloween.

To learn more about Jennifer B. White, log on to www.jenniferbwhite.com. You can follow her on Twitter @nakedhollywood where amazing celebrities, TV shows like E! and really cool organizations like Sundance Film Festival follow her. She's also on Facebook because she likes to post pictures of her food. Unlike a lot of mean people, Jennifer actually responds personally to all her emails and tweets.

Jennifer

www.ingramcontent.com/pod-product-compliance
Lightning Source LLC
Chambersburg PA
CBHW020405150626
46554CB00012B/272